UNDERGROUND
TO PALESTINE

UNDERGROUND TO PALESTINE

I. F. STONE

PANTHEON BOOKS, New York

Library of Congress Cataloging in Publication Data

Stone, Isidor F., 1907–
Underground to Palestine.

Reprint of the 1946 ed. published by Boni &
Gaer, New York, with new introd. and epilogue by
the author.
    1. World War, 1939–1945—Refugees. 2. World
War, 1939–1945—Jews. 3. Stone, Isidor, F.,
1907–   I. Title.
D808.S75 1978   940.53′159   78-65309
ISBN 0-394-50274-4
ISBN 0-394-73620-6 pbk.

Manufactured in the United States of America

FIRST EDITION

CONTENTS

NOTE: The YIVO Institute transliteration scheme for Yiddish is used throughout, except where transliteration is so well known as to be instantly recognizable, i.e., *chassid* and *challah.*

A Word in Preface
a Generation Later

The Second World War was like a giant earthquake which uprooted millions of Europeans. One scene I remember brought it all home to me in the autumn of 1945. In the battered railroad yards of Frankfurt-am-Main, I watched some of the worst railroad stock I have ever seen—half-wrecked freight cars and ancient third-class coaches jam-packed with refugees from the extermination camps of Nazi Germany. These were among the lucky few who had escaped starvation and the human furnaces. They exuded a joyful air, despite the grimy tatters they wore. The trains switched, some north, some south, some east, some west. They were going home. Looking on, one felt what the word meant to them. But still in the camps, now dubbed—anti-septically—"displaced persons' camps," were more than 100,000 Eastern and Central European Jews with no homes to return to. These were the other survivors of the Holocaust.

While the great powers in the newly organized United Nations debated and hesitated, none anxious to add to the ranks of their unemployed by opening their doors to the "displaced," these survivors began to move out of the camps in a more or less secret "underground to Palestine," and the British mustered a fleet in the Mediterranean to keep them out. This is the account of who they were and what they experienced by the first reporter to travel with these illegal emigrants through the British blockade. Appended to this new edition is the same reporter's reaction, thirty years later, to the plight and the moral challenge of the Arab refugees created in their wake.

June 1978

To
Those Anonymous Heroes
The *Shelikhim* of the *Haganah*

"The Germans killed us. The British don't let us live."—Jewish ex-Partisan.

In Explanation

This is a story of personal adventure. I was the first newspaper-man to travel the Jewish underground in Europe and to arrive in Palestine on a so-called illegal boat. But this is more than the narrative of a journalistic escapade. I am an American and I am also and inescapably—the world being what it is—a Jew. I was born in the United States. My parents were born in Russia. Had they not emigrated at the turn of the century to America, I might have gone to the gas chambers in Eastern Europe. I might have been a DP, ragged and homeless like those with whom I traveled. I did not go to join them as a tourist in search of the picturesque, nor even as a newspaperman merely in search of a good story, but as a kinsman, fulfilling a moral obligation to my brothers. I wanted in my own way, as a journalist, to provide a picture of their trials and their aspirations in the hope that good people, Jewish and non-Jewish, might be moved to help them.

I have not faked and I have not fictionalized except to hide the names of persons and places. I have not glossed over the unpleasant. My comrades of the voyage would be dishonored by anything less than the truth. I hope that, however inadequately, I may also have provided a record of some value to history. The clandestine exodus of the Jews from postwar Europe is the greatest in the history of a wandering people—greater than the exodus from Egypt or from Spain—because their sufferings under Hitler were greater than any our ancestors ever underwent before. We know comparatively little of the emigration from Egypt or of what went on aboard those tragic ships out of Spain which Columbus may have passed in 1492 on his way to a new world. This narrative may fill a humble gap in the annals of the current emigration. It was a privilege to take part in that emigration. I only wish I had the power to portray what I saw against the background of the world situation today. The plight of the Jews may be a minor affair. But world indifference to that plight is of spiritual significance for the future of us all.

I can only record as a reporter what I saw and heard, traveling with the least fortunate but the bravest of my people.

—April, 1946

Summons to Adventure

I

I was in the press gallery at Hunter College in the
Bronx when the call came. It was April, 1946. The
Security Council of the United Nations was in session.
The floodlighted scene below me seemed unreal, like the
setting for a play—perhaps a play about the fumbling of
the peace. Sir Alexander Cadogan, Britain's representative
at that horseshoe-shaped council table — a small man,
dapper and correct—was making a professionally astrin-
gent argument designed to prevent action against Franco.
An usher tapped me on the shoulder and said I was wanted
on the phone.

The interruption was not so irrelevant as it seemed at first. In Sir Alexander's subtle apologetics for a Fascist dictator, I had seen one aspect of the Empire's postwar policy. I was soon to see another. When I picked up the phone in one of the booths in the big press room in the basement, I heard the voice of an American I had met the preceding November in Palestine.

"How would you like to meet some boys who volunteered to serve as seamen for the illegal immigration?" he asked me. Neither of us realized on what a journey that question was to send me.

Of course I was interested. I had reason to believe that the man who phoned me was in close touch with the leaders of the *Haganah,* the Jewish people's militia of Palestine. I had heard many stories of its exploits during the war, when the *Haganah* directed underground rescue work in Hitler Europe. In April, 1946, a year after the liberation, the *Haganah* was back at much the same job, though under altered circumstances. The cruelty of the Nazis had given way to the indifference of the victors; the concentration camps had become DP camps. The Jews in them were still homeless.

Earl Harrison of Philadelphia had returned eight months before from a special tour of these camps to report at the White House, "We seem to be treating the Jews as the Nazis treated them, except that we do not exterminate them." President Truman had asked the British government to open the doors of Palestine to the 100,000 Jews in the displaced persons' camps of Germany and Austria before winter came, but the only result was an

Anglo-American Committee of Inquiry. It was spring and the committee had yet to make its report. A trickle of 1500 a month was entering Palestine legally under the limited immigration quota granted by the British, but the one hope of the rest was still the *Aliyah Beth.*

Aliyah is a Hebrew word which may be translated as "immigration," though its connotations are richer. Literally, the word means an "up-going," as to a high place; its associations are those of the pilgrimage. *Beth* in this context means "second," and distinguishes this immigration from the one allowed by the British. *Aliyah Beth* is the Palestinian term for what the British call the "illegal" immigration; the difference goes deeper than terminology.

This is a subject on which the British do not see eye to eye with the Jews. The Colonial Office looks back to the White Paper of 1939. Under its terms the doors of Palestine should be shut tight against further Jewish immigration. But to the Jews Palestine is still—as in the Bible — *Eretz Israel,* the land of Israel. To them the British are another of those historic vexations like the Assyrians and the Romans. From the Jewish point of view the White Paper is a violation of the Balfour Declaration; the whole affair—the 1917 promise and the 1939 breaking of it—a bit of latter-day presumption. For is it not written, of an older covenant with Abraham, "And He said unto him, I am the Lord that brought thee out of Ur of the Chaldees, to give thee this land to inherit it. . . . Unto thy seed have I given this land"?

This may, indeed, be theological nonsense and stubborn Jewish foolishness. Mr. Bevin and the gentlemen of the

Foreign Office and the Colonial Office may be right in dismissing it as such. But the Jews have been that way for a long time; they were that way long before there was a Britain; unconsciously they feel that way today.

I set all this down at the beginning of my story so that the reader will understand that when my American friend referred to the "illegal immigration" he did so only as a matter of convenience and that when he warned that the visit he suggested must be kept highly confidential, it was not as though he spoke of something shameful or furtive.

I said, "Call me back in fifteen minutes." I phoned my managing editor.

"John," I pleaded, "please let me have the rest of the day off for an expedition of my own. I may never be able to tell you about it, but I know you would agree it was worth while."

He tried to sound exasperated. "Go ahead, Izzy," he told me wearily. "You always were a mysterious guy. I suppose there's no use trying to hold you."

II

When my mysterious friend called back, I arranged to meet him at a railroad station in Manhattan. I took the Lexington Avenue subway downtown. I have never known the subway to go so slowly.

On my way downtown I thought of my visit to Palestine in November, 1945. The publication of the Harrison report the preceding autumn had sent me off on my first visit to the Holy Land. I had wanted to see the country for myself. Like most American Jews I was neither a Zionist nor an anti-Zionist. The problem of "displaced" European Jewry — what a gingerly understatement that adjective embodies! — and the reported desire of the majority to go to Palestine had awakened my interest. I went out to estimate for myself the possibility of rebuilding their lives in that country. I fell in love with the place, with its vitality and its pioneering spirit. I understood the motivations behind the Return. Now it seemed to me, as I impatiently watched the subway stations go by, that perhaps I might have the opportunity of seeing something of the other side of the picture, of catching some glimpse of the migration itself and the conditions behind it.

When I met my friend at the railroad station, I asked him impatiently, "Where are we going?"

He was in a happy mood. "You'll see," he said, and led me by the arm to a train. He had the pleased look of a small boy with a surprise up his sleeve. But I had a bigger surprise for him. An idea had begun to form in my mind on the way down.

Late that night in a city near New York I met a group of two dozen American Jewish boys who were preparing to sail for Europe the next day. There they would be sent to a Mediterranean port where they would board one of the illegal ships and prepare to take it through the British blockade and into Palestine.

"Until now," my friend told me proudly, "we had depended on professional sailors attracted by good pay for a dangerous mission. This ship will be the first to be manned by American Jewish boys who volunteered their services in a desire to help. Some are experienced sailors. Others are going to sea for the first time.

I was flattered when some of the boys recognized me and one said he had read my articles on Palestine in *PM* and the *Nation*. There were drinks all around and then I sprang *my* surprise.

"I'd like to go along," I told my Palestinian friend, "and write the whole story of the voyage from the beginning to the arrival in Palestine."

The boys were to sail the next day, and I said I was prepared to come back in the morning and sail with them. I said I was ready to board their illegal ship in Europe as newspaperman, passenger, crew member or stowaway— whichever was the most convenient. The proposal precipitated an argument.

Some liked the idea of having an official historian along on the voyage, especially those who were *PM* fans. Others feared that my presence might arouse suspicion in Europe.

It was finally agreed that I should be allowed to go along, but my American friend warned me that there was no point in my trying to sail next day with the boys. He warned me that they would have to wait four to eight weeks in Europe before an illegal ship and its passengers were ready for them.

"I suggest," he said, "that you wait until an illegal ship is ready to take on its cargo in Europe for Palestine.

You can then fly across to Europe in time to get on the
boat before it embarks for the voyage across the Mediterranean."

We all agreed that that would be the wiser plan. But
even this plan had to be somewhat tentative.

"We must tell you, however," my friend said, "that you
cannot be absolutely certain of making the trip. Final decision will have to rest with *Haganah* officials in Europe.
Circumstances might arise which would make it impossible for them to allow a newspaperman on one of the
ships. You might fly across and then find that you could
not embark after all."

I said I was willing to take the chance.

I was also warned that a great deal depended on my
discretion. No other newspaperman had ever been permitted to travel the underground route to Palestine. "Any
leak," I was told, "might be disastrous."

I told no one but my wife—the most discreet woman
I know—and the two top editors of *PM* what I was plan-
ning to do. My chief on the *Nation,* Freda Kirchwey, was
out of the country at the time, herself on the way to Palestine. I hoped my other colleagues on the *Nation* would for-
give me for telling them that I was taking a leave of ab-
sence to cover the Paris Peace Conference for *PM.*

I applied for and obtained my passport, but getting a
visa from the British for Palestine was a problem. I intended to go without a visa if the British refused to grant
me one. At the British Embassy in Washington, the official
in charge wanted to know what I intended to do as a newspaperman in Palestine. Was I, he inquired delicately, go-

ing to cover the—uh—Arabs or was I going to cover the
—uh—Jews? I pretended not to understand. I said it was
a small country and that to get a real story I'd have to
cover both.

The answer didn't satisfy him. He said I'd have to give
him $25 to cover the cost of a cable to the British infor-
mation officer in Jerusalem, presumably to ask whether I
was *persona grata*. The British don't like newspapermen
around their empire who fail to absorb the British point
of view. I remembered the troubles my friend, Constantine
Poulos, of Overseas News Agency had encountered in the
Middle East after he had sent a dispatch comparing British
actions in Palestine with their conduct in Greece, and I recalled also the difficulties which had piled up for the late
Ben Robertson of *PM* when he failed to see eye to eye with
the British on India. I told the Embassy visa officer that I
couldn't wait while he consulted the British authorities in
Jerusalem on my acceptability.

I went around to see a high official of the Embassy, a
gentle and scholarly Tory, who gave me my visa at once
after telling me pointedly that of course the British, unlike
the Russians, did not intend to hide behind an iron curtain. I thanked him. (When I got back I gathered that the
poor chap was in hot water with the Foreign Office for his
devotion to freedom of the press. Almost my first call on
my return to America was from my friend, Charlie Camp-
bell, the chief British information officer in Washington,
saying that London wanted to know how I had gotten my
visa.)

I spent an impatient month around Washington. The

day finally arrived when I got word that it was time to leave for Europe. It was the middle of May when I took off from La Guardia Field and headed for the North Atlantic.

III

I landed at Hurn airport the next day. From the train window on the two-and-a-half-hour ride to London, rural England had the appearance of a well kept garden. The cottages with their hedgerows, the green rolling downs, the dull yellow of the neat haycocks delighted the eye.

London was scarred and pitted. There were jagged edges in the skyline of chimney pots and palaces. Along the docks of the East End I saw whole blocks blasted and leveled. In the busy West End there was hardly a street that did not have some reminder of the blitz. Empty spaces gaped from among the buildings and weeds had begun to spring up in the rubble. There were buildings which seemed whole but turned out to be blind and hollow shells, their innards torn away.

In this dowager of imperial cities with its antique charm there was a reluctant admiration for, but also an undercurrent of resentment against America. American movies were everywhere, as were imitations of American advertising methods. But the contrast between Britain's continuing hardships and American prosperity was not made easier to bear by our own failure to meet food commitments to

Europe. America, to the meagerly fed Englishman, was a
place where greedy folk ate ten meals a day.

I found these feelings reflected in the average Englishman's resentment over what he regarded as American inter-
ference in the Palestine problem. The British were sensitive about charges of imperialism, and in no mood to be
preached to by America on imperial problems. No important country is as dependent as theirs on imports. To the
ordinary Britisher at the moment the Empire meant the
sterling bloc and the sterling bloc meant bread and butter.

The Englishman felt that his country was more generous than America in taking refugees during the Hitler period and the war. He regarded his standards of race toler-
ance as higher than our own. Palestine had been a British
mandate, Zionism a British political issue, since the last
war. There was great sentimental interest in the problem
of a Jewish national home.

But at that moment, with a hundred and one (for him)
far more urgent problems on his hands, the average Britisher was in no mood for risks in the Middle East. He had
been sold the idea that further concessions to the Jews on
Palestine would "inflame" the Arab world and he felt he
had troubles enough without Arab uprisings.

In the noisy crowded bar of the House of Commons, one
sensed that the Conservatives were resigned, the Laborites
jubilant, over the current pledge to withdraw from Egypt.
It was felt that the new White Paper on India was the
answer to "nonsense" about the "continuity of foreign policy from the Tory to the Labor regime." But the plan to
withdraw from Egypt seemed to have made the British

Government more intent than ever on keeping Palestine as a military base in the Middle East.

The Anglo-American Committee of Inquiry had just made its report on Palestine, unanimously recommending the admission of the 100,000 DP's from the German and Austrian camps and the ultimate establishment of a binational Arab-Jewish state in Palestine. I talked at the House of Commons one night with Richard H. S. Crossman, a Labor MP and one of the editors of the London *New Statesman and Nation.* Crossman's sympathy and courage as a member of the committee had been the principal factor in winning the British members to these unexpected unanimous recommendations. He was staking his political future in the Labor Party on the Palestine issue. I verified in London what Bartley J. Crum, the most militant American member of the committee, had charged in the United States—that Foreign Minister Ernest Bevin at a farewell luncheon to the committee in London had given his word that the British Government would put into effect any unanimous recommendations by the committee. It was already clear at the time I was in London that Bevin had no intention of keeping his promise.

I left London feeling that Jewish refugees could expect little sympathy from the average Englishman, and even less from the British Government. I was anxious to get on and see what the Jews could do for themselves, and took a boat train for the Continent.

IV

The city to which I was directed is one of the loveliest on the Continent, but the people seemed hungry and cold. There were no taxis, and I paid two hundred francs to an extraordinarily thin but very intelligent porter who carried my bags to the hotel. I had been given instructions on how to make contact with an underground *Haganah* worker. The method was rather roundabout. My second day I received word to be at a certain café at seven o'clock that evening.

I was sitting outside the café at that hour, enjoying the passing crowds, when a man tapped me on the shoulder and asked me if I was I. F. Stone. I said I was and asked him if his name was Jacques. My friend was the *sheliakh* I had been told to contact.

The word *sheliakh* in Hebrew means "emissary." It is applied to every sort of representative sent abroad by a Palestinian Jewish organization, but is used more especially for those men assigned by the *Haganah* for underground rescue and illegal immigration work in Europe.

I will not do the British Intelligence Service the favor of describing Jacques too closely. I came to know him well during my stay abroad. He was a cultured person with a sense of fun and adventure, but at the same time a man of tremendous devotion to the task assigned him. If you can imagine Galahad with a sense of humor you'll get a pretty good spiritual picture of my friend—in fact those few people who know the underground workers in Europe will recognize him at once from that description. I must say I have never met a nobler group of human beings than the *shelikhim* I encountered abroad.

In almost all Jewish organizations operating in Europe, as in almost all social welfare groups, a certain unpleasant and bureaucratic atmosphere is evident. An invisible wall grows up between the people to be helped and those doing the helping. I never felt any attitude of superiority, condescension or patronage toward refugees among the *Haganah* men working in the *Aliyah Beth*.

Many were men of wide education and experience. Some had led lives of quiet scholarship before the war. Others were members of farm collectives in Palestine. They had stories to tell which cannot yet be published. Few people have ever been fortunate enough to be served by men of such ability and consecration to their task.

I was happy to learn from Jacques that I would be allowed to make the trip. I did not yet know how many difficulties still lay ahead of me.

"We have decided," the *Haganah* worker told me, "to let you travel as a passenger on an *Aliyah Beth* boat and to write about your experiences providing you use as few real names as possible of people and places. The British are making it harder for us every day to go on with our rescue work."

I was disappointed to learn that I would not be able to board a boat immediately.

"The *Aliyah Beth*," the *Haganah* worker told me with

a smile, "is far from being as well organized as a Cook's tour. The greatest exodus in the history of the Jewish people is under way in Europe. Refugees are seeping through every border in a desperate effort to get out of this hate-infested continent to Palestine. We're doing the best we can to help them, but that best is all too little. The one thing they cannot do unaided is to cross the Mediterranean, and that is where our major task comes in. But there are interminable difficulties and unforeseen delays. I don't know how soon I can get you on a ship."

The *Haganah* worker suggested that I spend a week acquiring visas for every country in the Mediterranean.

"The next ship may be leaving from France, or Italy, or Yugoslavia, or Greece, or Rumania. You'd better be prepared to fly to any one of those countries on a few hours' notice," he advised.

But after a week of visa gathering I still found myself with no sailing in prospect.

It was not easy to reach that *Haganah* worker. I had a telephone number but it was only that of a friendly businessman who in turn had to contact a third person who by roundabout ways forwarded messages to the *Haganah*. I was growing impatient and sought another meeting. When I finally managed to get in touch with the *Haganah* worker with whom I had first spoken, he suggested that I have a look at the DP camps in Germany and Austria, and then go on into Czechoslovakia, and, if there was still time, Poland.

"You might as well see for yourself," he said, "what conditions lie behind this migration."

I asked whether I might travel back from Poland via the underground. He warned against it.

"Conditions in Poland are very unsettled and Jews are often shot at by bandit or anti-Semitic gangs on their way out," he told me. "It would be better to come out by plane."

The *Haganah* worker gave me a list of underground contacts in Germany, Austria, Czechoslovakia and Poland, and he wrote out a kind of passport in Hebrew, saying that I was a newspaperman who could be trusted. I went to Paris and obtained temporary military orders for Germany from U. S. Army headquarters at the Hotel Majestic and filed an application at the Polish Embassy in Paris for a visa to Poland. Then I left on the Orient Express for Germany.

I See the DP's

I

Of Germany my first impressions were the rubble of the cities and the untouched rich green of the countryside. Crossing the Rhine on the train from Strasbourg into the French zone, I saw a wrecked bridge and then at Kehl, a ruined railroad station. On the platform lounged a few German prisoners in dirty dungarees and several French soldiers with red stripes down the side of their blue pants, like the toy soldiers we played with as children.

All along the line, at every station and in every town, the railroad stations were battered, houses gutted. But despite all I saw on the way, to walk out of the railroad sta-

18

tion in the lowering dusk of a rainy evening in Munich was unexpectedly macabre. The railway plaza looked like a scene from the H. G. Wells movie *Things To Come*. All that was left of the few buildings which lined the plaza were a few crazy brick skeletons, on one of which, high up, an undamaged bathtub protruded dizzily from a precarious bit of wall. Through the broken windows I could see the darkening sky. Piles of wreckage exuded the smell of un-buried bodies. The trams still ran, people moved about like ants in a ruined anthill, temporary booths at the station provided permits for the few taxis and also ration cards for *Wurst-Butter-Käse* [sausage, butter, and cheese], but these evidences of life only made Munich seem all the more like some dreadful nightmare.

Ninety miles north in medieval Nuremberg, where the old walled city lay half ruined, the war crimes trial ground on. I was there for a morning to see the impatience of the dignified British chief justice, Lawrence, and to hear him say "Get on, get on," irritably, at the awkward cross-exami-nation and interminable leading questions of the clumsy German defense lawyers. I heard Baldur von Schirach, the Nazi youth leader, explain that he was one of the Jews' best friends. And as I watched that odd collection of shifty German burgers on trial, pasty faced and shabby, it seemed to me that the ex-Supermen might have been a group of middle aged, pompous German respectables caught in a raid on some shady establishment.

In the voluminous testimony through which I leafed with *PM's* Victor Bernstein, I was struck by one vivid pas-sage. It was in the testimony of Rudolph Hess, the former commandant of Auschwitz. Of the gas chambers he said, "We knew when the people were dead because they stopped screaming." Of the panic on the way to the chambers: "Very frequently women would hide their children under their clothes, but of course when we found them we would send the children in to be exterminated."

II

Into this Germany of destruction, death, and dreadful memories, Jews were pouring from Eastern Europe to wait an opportunity to get to Palestine. It was ironical and dangerous that Germany should be the one country in Europe in which the Jewish population was growing constantly, and serious trouble was possible there. The hatred of the Jews for the Germans—in each of whom they saw the murderer of parents, wives, and children—was not difficult to imagine, though the most objective and dispassionate view of the German problem I heard in the Reich was from a seventeen-year-old Lithuanian Jewish boy I met on a truck going to Landsberg. He did not regard the Germans as a lost people but as one badly poisoned. He thought that given a long and wisely handled occupation they could be rehabilitated and fitted into the framework of a decent and progressive Europe. But I did not get this calm view from most of the DP's with whom I talked.

The Germans themselves, obsequious or sullen, gave me little sense of change and the few German progressives with whom I talked, though they voiced optimistic views, betrayed their fear that they would be back in jail or concentration camp again if and when the occupying powers left.

In Nuremberg I saw Social Democratic wall posters pleading *"Deutsche Mütter! Wollt ihr jemals wieder eure Söhne dem Krieg opfern?"* [German mothers! Do you wish ever again to sacrifice your sons to war?] But one wondered whether some would not answer "yes" instead of the "nein" with which the placard urged them to vote the Social Democratic ticket. In tiny Amberg I heard a communist leader admit that Nazism had eaten *"tief, sehr tief"* [deep, very deep] into the German working class and that only a long occupation could re-educate these people. In the meantime it was easier for the Germans to fall back on the old scapegoat: "The Jews are the cause of our misfortune," those fierce creatures streaming in from the East who were not afraid to beat up the German policemen who ventured into their camps. The American zone of Germany, with its hundred thousand restless Jews, still homeless and still far from free a year and a half after the liberation, seemed a human volcano in which bloody battles might break out at any time and spread from town to town.

Here a whole group of agencies were trying to do their best with a difficult and growing problem. The United States Army, UNRRA, and the Joint Distribution Committee had the job of providing homes, food, and clothing. Some of the camps, especially the transient centers, were dreadful and dirty places. I visited one such center, run by UNRRA in a bombed-out Luftwaffe Signal Corps factory in Funk Caserne outside Munich. This was a reception and repatriation camp which had handled people of fifty-five different nationalities on their way home, including folk from as far as Ethiopia, Afghanistan, and Saudi Arabia. The stream of other nationalities was tapering off, but fifteen hundred Jews a month were still coming through there.

The harassed UNRRA staff did its best; I saw two truckloads of children, including small girls in braids, go off from the camp to a puppet show while I was there. Gardens had been planted and I was proudly shown the spotless white tile hospital built by the DP's themselves. But sleeping quarters for the transients were still in a huge and stinking third floor loft with three tiers of bunks. The center had room for twenty-three hundred transients, who were moved out to permanent camps as rapidly as possible.

"If conditions here were too good," one of my UNRRA guides said, "they'd stay on. This is only supposed to be a clearance center."

Jewish life in Germany was strange and full of contrasts. Not a half hour's drive from these filthy barracks which housed transient Jews at Funk Caserne, I visited the American Military Government headquarters in Munich. I was in the office of a former German Jewish refugee who had escaped before the war, gone to America, enlisted in the United States Army after Pearl Harbor, become a captain and been assigned to military government in his native land. He was a big fellow; his anteroom was full of admiring German *Fräulein* assistants and secretaries whom he seemed to keep in a constant flutter. He appeared half American, half Prussian. He was enjoying himself tremendously and his reverberating *Jawohls* on the telephone sounded like those of an old-fashioned Junker officer, tremendously pleased with himself and his authority.

III

Conditions in the permanent camps varied considerably. The prize exhibit of the lot was the famous *kibbutz* on the farm once owned by the notorious Nazi anti-Semitic publisher, Streicher, near Nuremberg. There, amid the green rolling Franconian hills, DP's lived much the same life they would live in Palestine. I saw them bring the cows home at evening. I talked with their chief agronomist, Josef Heler, a Polish Jewish farmer from Galicia on the Russian side of the Ribbentrop-Molotov line, who was sent to a labor camp in Siberia as a *kulak* and freed after the Stalin-Sikorski agreement. He became assistant director of a ten-thousand-hectare beet-sugar farm near Djamboul in Kazakstan. His wife and two children were killed by the Germans during the invasion. The Russians wanted him to stay in Kazakstan, but gave him his papers as a Polish citizen repatriate when he insisted on leaving.

"I was well treated and had useful work in Kazakstan," Heler said, "but I left because having suffered as a Jew I

wanted to live as a Jew. I'm going to Palestine where I
think my experience with similar agricultural conditions in
arid Kazakstan will be very useful."

The communal kitchen, the simple dinner of sour cream,
bread and butter, fresh vegetables, and coffee, the singing
of the *khalutsim,* reminded me of the colonies I had visited
in Palestine in 1945. Heler told me that they not only
raised all their own food but supplied milk to nearby DP
camps.

"What about meat?" I asked him.

"Come, I'll show you," he said with an amused gleam
in his eye.

He took me to the huge barns where he proudly showed
me two of the biggest sows I have ever seen.

"Not exactly *kosher,*" he said, "but very tasty."

The largest camp I visited, one of the largest in Germany, was at the little Bavarian town of Landsberg in
whose medieval fortress Hitler was imprisoned after the
1923 Munich beer-hall putsch. Here one saw a typical
group of DP's—*"die zweite Kategorie der Menschen"* [the
second class of mankind], as one of the DP's there wryly
described them to me. The camp was a collection of brick
buildings in a kind of compound which had once been
used as an artillery plant. What I first saw there was a lot
of ill-dressed Jews walking about in a rather dispirited and
desultory way in the courtyard. They were an unattractive
lot. I walked through them to the main building—which
has been renamed Roosevelt House—where I found the
telephone operator in her cubbyhole at the entrance reading Henrietta Buckmaster's story of the slave South, *Deep*

River. The operator was a Polish Jewish girl, a DP, who read English better than she spoke it. In the building was a library, offices of various agencies and committees, and meeting rooms. The operator put me in touch with an UNRRA official who took me around.

The people in this camp seemed to fall into three groups. One was made up of pretty bad elements, people who had been hurt morally by the things they had to do to survive. Among them were black marketeers and petty speculators. They were a minority. A second group was made up of those who had little stamina left. They were living out of their suitcases as it were, anxious to go as soon as they could. In the meantime it was hard to get them to do much of anything. A third group was of people who were just as anxious to leave as the others but prepared to spend their time usefully while they waited. Among them were people of natural leadership and ability who organized schools and workshops and helped to train their fellows for a useful life elsewhere. Almost all of them wanted to go to Palestine.

Getting things done at Landsberg was often a challenge to ingenuity. The camp officials and the more enterprising DP's wanted to build a brick wall at the entrance.

"We couldn't get any bricks," one official told me, "so we had to tear down a brick air-raid shelter. To use these old bricks, we had to have special tools. We couldn't buy tools so we had to make them in our own workshop. But to make tools of raw metal, we had to have coke. To get the coke we pulled a deal with German officials in the town, swapped some things they wanted for the coke we needed."

I visited the schools at Landsberg and talked with the DP's who had helped to organize them. One of them was a young Polish engineer named Wolf Michelski. He was twenty-eight, slight of build and dark haired. He was from Kovno in Lithuania. He had been a construction engineer in his home town. His mother, sister, and father went to their deaths when the Germans liquidated the Kovno ghetto in 1944, but he was sent to a work camp in Stutthoff and later to Landsberg. There he worked in the artillery factory that now houses the DP's.

"Eighteen hundred able bodied Jews from the Kovno ghetto were sent to the German work camps," Michelski said, "but only four hundred survived.

"After the liberation we took equipment from the factory and began to organize a trade school. We repaired the old smithy, and now use it for metal work."

Michelski proudly showed me the smithy and the workshops adjoining it. The prize equipment was a mechanical saw and an electric planing machine. They had a carpenter's shop, a welding department and a radio school in which the students did all kinds of repair work for the camp.

"We teach fourteen different trades here," Michelski told me. "We have budding locksmiths, carpenters, shoemakers, tailors, dental technicians, photographers, radio repair men, electricians, auto mechanics, chauffeurs, farmers, and male nurses, and we hope soon to inaugurate a course for aviation mechanics."

Another of the leading personalities among the DP's in Landsberg was a young Polish Jew of thirty, Joe Buda, who

spoke good "American" English and from contact with
American soldiers had acquired the look and ways of a
typical GI. He was energetic, sandy haired, of medium
height. Joe was from Lodz, where his father owned a textile factory. He had an engineering degree from a Belgian
technical school where he studied from 1934 to 1938. He
had returned to Lodz to work as technical and engineering
director of his father's factory until the Germans came and
ordered all the Lodz Jews into a ghetto.

"I was betrothed," Joe told me, "and when the Germans
established the ghetto in Lodz my fiancée and I ran away
to Warsaw where we were married. The Germans put us
into a work camp. We ran away. For a time we hid in the
ghetto, and for a while we found work of a sort in the railway station at Warsaw. In 1942 the Germans caught me
and my wife again and sent us to Maidenek. We were separated. My wife was put in Field No. 4; I was put in Field
No. 5. We did no more than catch glimpses of each other
in the six months we were there. The last I saw of my wife
was when I managed to throw a kiss to her as I was being
taken away with other able-bodied men to a new work
place. She tried hard not to cry and so did I. I later heard
that she was sent to the gas chambers. None of my family
is left."

Joe and the man who taught dental technique at the
Landsberg camp took me on a memorable visit to a former
concentration camp nearby. The dentist's name was Dr.
Abel Akabas; he was a sturdy, dignified looking man from
Kovno, Lithuania. He had been an inmate of this concen-
tration camp, known as Lager No. 2, and he was one of the

few who had survived. He survived because he was a dentist. It was his job to pull the gold teeth from the mouths of the dead, "sometimes," he told me grimly, "from heads without bodies." The gold was collected by the Nazis at the camp.

The camp was hidden away in a lovely emerald green forest off the main road to Landsberg. It was about a hundred yards square, surrounded by barbed wire. Inside were the bunkers in which the Jews lived. These were a kind of dugout, as long as a house and several feet underground, with peaked wooden roofs over them on which earth had been piled for warmth and on which grass grew.

Dr. Akabas took me to the dugout bunker in which he lived. Across the entrance was the derisive name "Sommerfreude" [summer joy]. One had to stoop to enter. It was about five hundred feet square.

"About three hundred men lived in here, if you can call it living," Dr. Akabas told me; "about twenty-five died every day."

Our audience in the bunker was made up of four cows who looked at us with gentle, melancholy eyes. The concentration camp was already in use. A German woman lived in what had been the commander's house and stabled her cows in these bunkers where men had lived and died. She was a short, dumpy, irascible woman whose only reaction to our visit was to walk up angrily after we had left and slam the wire covered door behind us. We had forgotten to shut it firmly.

IV

It was a visit to a DP camp at Furth near Nuremberg
that helped me to understand vividly just how difficult it
was to live in these camps in Germany. The camp I visited
was run by a Major Cummings who worked for UNRRA.
He was a stocky but dapper little Australian. He had fought
in the Australian Army in the First World War, worked
for the Anglo-Iranian Oil Company between the two wars,
and served in the British Middle East command during the
Second World War. To judge only by that brief record
one might expect a rather unsympathetic person, with the
anti-Jewish prejudices some Britishers get in the Middle
East. But Major Cummings was one of the finest human
beings I met during my entire trip, a competent executive
and at the same time an extraordinarily kind and understanding man.

You could judge the morale of a DP camp at once by
its cleanliness or lack of it. This camp outside Furth was
clean. There were curtains and flowerpots in the windows
of the houses in the camp, a sure sign of good morale.
Many of the people were orthodox Jews from Carpatho-
Russia in what was Eastern Czechoslovakia and is now
part of the Soviet Union. They had a synagogue and were
building themselves a theater. Outside the commissary
and the bakery, which smelled of fresh bread, was a notice
in Yiddish and English explaining the rationing system

in the camp and the amounts of food available per person.

"We try to explain everything to the people here," Major Cummings told me. "Things work out better if they know exactly what's going on."

He showed me the gardens in which the DP's raised their own vegetables. At one point I began talking to a group of refugees and asked what they would do about the German problem. It was a bad question. They got pretty excited. Afterward at lunch Major Cummings said: "You know they're a very emotional people." The average Englishman, brought up in the tradition of emotional restraint, would have said it in a tone of superiority, probably with contempt. Major Cummings said it in a fatherly way, as one who did not wish me to get a bad impression of the people in his charge.

I went around the camp by myself, looking into the various apartments and talking with people. They were clean and in good condition. In one apartment I talked with a Polish Jew, a former textile worker from Lodz, which was a center of the Polish textile industry. Unlike so many of the Polish Jews he was not undersized but a healthy and vigorous looking man. He told me he had lost his family and he praised the camp and its director.

"It's one of the best camps in Germany," he said, "and we couldn't have a more understanding director. But it's still no home."

He added a sentence that hit me hard.

"When I look out my window," he confided, "and see the barbed wire, *es vert mir kalt in hartsen* [my heart grows cold] and when I go with my *tepele* [my little

pot] to get my meals, I feel as though I'm still in *KZ* [pro-
nounced *ka-tset,* German abbreviation for concentration
camp]."

V

I think I learned most about Germany when I got lost
on my way from Nuremberg to Czechoslovakia and went
to Amberg instead of Bamberg. I didn't know a soul in
the town and the signs pointing to PRO, which I took
joyfully to mean the Press Relations Officer, led only to a
prophylactic station. I was traveling on Army orders and
in military correspondent's uniform, so I was given a billet
at the little officers' club. I set out to explore the town. It
is what one would have described sentimentally two dec-
ades ago as a Hans Christian Andersen kind of town until
we all learned what horrors can come out of these quaint
little places with their ancient churches, arched bridges,
and the stork nests on their chimneys.

It was evening and I walked down the main street to
the town hall which is now the American Military Government headquarters. Nearby, as though for safety, were
a Social Democratic party headquarters which was closed,
and a Communist party headquarters which was open. I
went in to have a look at the pamphlets on display in the
window and bought a set of them. One was an illustrated
pamphlet on Buchenwald and its horrors. Another was on
the war guilt of the German Reich and the *Mitschuld* of

the German people. [*Mitschuld* meaning, literally, the *guilt* that the people *shared* with their government.]

There were three men in the combination party head-quarters and bookshop. One of them seemed to be the communist leader of the town. I began to understand how many communists managed to survive under Hitler. They survived by abstaining from political activity. One of the men, an engineer, had been in jail four months as a political prisoner at the beginning of the Hitler period and afterwards was kept under surveillance. He had to report to the police regularly and was permitted only manual labor jobs. He was warned not to try to work in any arms plants, and he told me frankly that he had been able to do no political work. The one who seemed to be the leader spent a year and two months in Dachau for giving out anti-Nazi leaflets, and also lived by avoiding any political activity afterwards.

He told me that Amberg and its vicinity was rightist territory. Forty per cent of the people could not vote because they had been Nazis, and two-thirds of the remainder had voted the right wing Christian Socialist party ticket at the local elections. Thirty per cent voted Social Democratic and one per cent Communist. He complained that the AMG officers were partial to this right wing party but admitted that if the Americans left, the Germans would probably have the communists and socialists in jail again in a year or so. He felt that only a long occupation could change the character of the people.

I asked him whether he thought Jews could now live in Germany.

"Es ist sehr schlecht [It's very bad]," he answered.

He didn't think there was much hope of re-establishing Jews in Germany for a long time. I asked how many Jews were left in that town and he told me only forty. One of the communists offered to take me to their synagogue.

When I got there I found not local Jews but Polish Jewish refugees. They lived together in the community center and most of them were in the courtyard when I entered. The synagogue had been newly rebuilt thanks to help from the American Army, and its sacred utensils had been returned by a German who took them and hid them when the synagogue was burned in 1938. Upstairs they had a common mess hall, sleeping quarters and a library with a very old collection of books in English, Yiddish, and Hebrew, including *The Education of Henry Adams* and several dialogues of Plato. In the office of this center there were two pictures. One, a small one, was a picture of Theodore Herzl, the Viennese journalist who founded the Zionist movement. The other, a very large picture, was a picture of their hero and messiah, Sergeant M. Rubinoff of Portland, Maine. Sergeant Rubinoff, who had a round, good-natured Jewish boy's face, was the first American Jewish soldier to get into the town. He found seventy-five Jews in an UNRRA tuberculosis sanatorium, got them food and clothing and helped rebuild the synagogue. He still sent them letters and packages from Portland.

Two of the Polish Jews took me to visit the last remaining German Jew in Amberg and its surrounding territory.

We went up a narrow alley into a medieval house with earthen floor, up three rickety flights of stairs to an apartment in which we found a seventy-six year old Jewish woman, Clara Lorsch, having a bit of gingerbread with a middle aged German woman who was one of her neighbors. She was born, she told me in a creaking voice, in Steinach an der Saale, but had lived forty years in Amberg where she had a small shop. She was a widow. She remembered with gratitude that when the local Nazi commissar closed her shop up and confiscated its goods in 1938, he first granted her request to be allowed to take out linens for her own use and that of her daughter-in-law, who was now dead. She also remembered that even after 1938 her neighbors had greeted her in the streets when they saw her. Once a peasant woman gave her food. In 1941 she was sent to Theresienstadt and spent three years in a concentration camp. The old lady had a wry sense of humor.

"I have become the miracle of Amberg," she said, referring to the interest in her as the only native German Jew in that area.

She was leaving to spend her last years with her son, Dr. K. F. Lorsch, a London physician, whom she had not seen for many years.

Her neighbor, whom she had called in to share the gingerbread she had made, was very ingratiating and obsequious to us. But every once in a while this thin, spinsterish German woman would steal a glance at the two dark Polish Jews with me, a look of fascinated horror as though she expected rape at any moment, as in the passage in *Mein Kampf* about the dark Jew lying in wait for the blond Aryan maiden.

My last memory of Amberg and of Germany was the chat I had with the bartender in the officers' club that night. He showed me his *Wehrmacht* [German army] papers. He was a nice person and he pleaded that the German people must have "work and bread." But at the end of our talk he shook his head sadly and said in German:

"If he [meaning Hitler] came again and screamed, they'd follow him like sheep once more."

Underground Railway
to Bratislava

I

I had been visiting frontier posts and had reached the railroad station just in time. I ducked under the gates at the crossing, ran across the tracks, and jumped on the rear car. It was 4:25 on a June afternoon in a little Czech town near the Polish border. I will call it Anton.

I had arrived there only that morning. From sleepy Amberg in Germany I had made my way to Schwandorf and Furth-i-Wald, thence over the Czech border to Pilsen and Prague. In gloomy, medieval Prague the Polish Embassy had no word from Warsaw on my application for a visa. I decided to make my way to the Polish-Czech border, in the hope of joining a group of refugees on the border and traveling with them on the underground route to Palestine.

I had been lucky. I found myself at one of the most popular crossing points on the Polish-Czech frontier on the very day a transport was about to leave for Bratislava. In that Slovak capital a hundred and eighty miles to the southeast, they hoped to cross the Austrian frontier illegally into the Russian zone and proceed from there to Vienna.

I wore the military correspondent's uniform which I had acquired in the American military zone in Germany. The Czechs lounging on the station platform looked surprised to see an American in uniform swinging aboard that last car. Its grimy windows and decrepit appearance set it off unmistakably from the rest of the train.

I was traveling light and had only a briefcase and a brown canvas zipper bag. I heard someone on the last car shout in Yiddish: "Look, the American is coming with us!" Friendly hands grabbed my bags and helped me up into that ancient wooden third-class carriage. It was about one-third the size of an American railroad car and it was packed with Jewish refugees. They had seen me earlier in the day at the Czech Red Cross hospital through which they clear. They recognized me and I was greeted with *sholom*s [literally, in Hebrew, *peace*—the equivalent of our *hello*].

The car we were in had the European style side aisle, compartments with long wooden seats and one small washroom with a tap from which no water ran. The car

was dirty and crowded. Later, when I counted my fellow
passengers, I found there were fifty-five of us. All but two
were Jewish refugees who had managed to make their
way across the border from Poland into Czechoslovakia;
among them were fourteen women and four small children, the youngest three, the oldest ten. A Czech and I
were the other two.

The Czech, a thin friendly man in his fifties, told me
he was a member of the secret police. He had been assigned by the Czech Government to see us to our next
destination, Bratislava, the capital of Slovakia, about one
hundred and eighty miles to the southwest. His job was
to see that none of us got off the train before then, and,
I suppose, to keep order if necessary. He was half guard,
half escort. He told me, in a talk we had during the night,
that he served in the Czech Legion during the First World
War.

I had hardly caught my breath in the aisle before I was
approached by fellow passengers. They examined the
correspondent's patch on my shoulder and at once wanted
to know if the *Herr Korrespondent* knew their uncle in
"Jigago" or their cousin so-and-so in "Nefyork." Would
I take their names and the names of their relatives in
America for my paper? I promised I would.

As soon as the train began to move, everybody began
to sing. The first song whose words I could make out was
a Yiddish song written by a young man I was to meet
soon. It was called *"Khalutsim, Greyten Zikh Far Eretz
Israel"* ["Pioneers Prepare Themselves for Palestine"]. The
singing was spontaneous and joyful.

I was aware of the trials which lay ahead. I had seen some of the thousands waiting in the DP camps of Austria and Germany. I knew of the endless and exasperating diplomatic negotiations between America and Britain over the admission of one hundred thousand to Palestine. I had heard of the dangers and delays which beset the underground route to Palestine, but there was no apprehension among my fellow voyagers. They felt themselves on their way.

Behind were the green hills of the treacherous Polish-Czech border. Ahead somewhere were security, freedom, and a new home. Their determination and confidence infected me. It is only in retrospect that I feel the anxieties we should have felt that day as we started off from Anton.

I was rescued from the importunate address bearers by two young *khalutsim* who wanted me to sit with them. They picked up my bags and made a seat for me in one of the compartments. There were ten *khalutsim* in it, youngsters in their teens and early twenties, and an older man in his thirties, a Polish Jew with a mandolin.

Khalutsim means *pioneers* in Hebrew and is the term for people who have been in training for life in a settlement in Palestine. They are the Zionist élite, dedicated to the building of Palestine. The ten I was with, five boys and five girls, had all trained for several months in the same *kibbutz* [collective training settlement] in Poland. It was a *kibbutz* near Lodz called *Dror* [Freedom], supported by funds of the Poale Zion, the Labor Zionist movement.

As our train rattled along over the Czech countryside,

past green farms and tiny villages, the *khalutsim* told me of the trouble they had had getting across the border. Their experience was an unusual one. They were the only group I encountered in all my travels whose difficulties had occurred on the Czech rather than the Polish side of the border. A friendly Pole led them across the Polish frontier. Unfortunately they reached the Czech side not at the hospitable town of Anton, but about twenty-five miles away in a small Czech city where the police ordered them back to Poland.

The *khalutsim* told the police: "You can shoot us but you can't force us to go back into Poland." They were a ragged but determined lot of youngsters, and the Czech police must have realized that they meant it. The guards let them in and put them on a train for the clearance center at Anton, but they had to change trains halfway there, and at the halfway point the conductor wouldn't let them on the next train because they had no tickets and no money. The police at the station again ordered them back to Poland, and again they challenged the police: "You can shoot us, but we're not going back." The police finally put them on another train and told the conductor to let them ride free to Anton. There they found their way to the Red Cross hospital.

Twenty-five miles away from Anton, our train stopped at a local station and I could see that we were in for a long, slow ride. The locomotive was a museum piece that looked as if it would burst its boilers if it went faster than twenty miles an hour. I got out with some of the others to stretch my legs on the platform and began talking to the man with the mandolin.

The man with the mandolin was not a *khaluts*. He was a leather worker from Sosnowice in Poland. He had been a *Mizrachi* [conservative, religious] Zionist before the war and was on his way to Palestine. He told me his story, and he told it in the matter-of-fact way all the refugees I met spoke of their personal tragedies. For them, the hurt was too deep and familiar for tears.

"There were twenty-five hundred Jews in Sosnowice before the war," he said. "There are very few left now. Shortly after the Germans came, they sent us all into a ghetto. There my wife and I worked for the Gestapo as tailors. We had a six-year-old daughter.

"In 1943 the Germans liquidated the ghetto. All but three thousand able-bodied workers were sent away, as we discovered later, to be burned in the crematoriums. My wife and child were among them. I went with the workers to Auschwitz and later to Buchenwald."

He showed me the tattooed concentration camp number on his arm, 134571. I saw few Jewish arms in Europe without a tattooed number. The Jews show it to you proudly as a badge of honor.

"When my wife and child were sent away," the man continued, "my wife cried out to me: *'Mayn tayere* [my dear], when the war is over come look for us.' After those of us who survived were liberated from Buchenwald, I went back to Poland to see if I could find any trace of my wife and child. All I located was a sister-in-law who told me she had seen them on their way to the death furnaces."

When we were back in the train and had started off again, I asked him where he got the mandolin. He said that when the Germans sent him to the ghetto, he gave the mandolin for safekeeping to the Polish janitor of the apartment house in which he and his wife had lived. When he got back to Sosnowice he looked up the janitor, recovered his mandolin and started off on the road to Palestine.

"This," he said in Yiddish, "is all that remains of my old life."

So he played and the *khalutsim* sang.

II

Before boarding the train, my comrades had succeeded in getting over one of the most dangerous frontiers in Eastern Europe.

By day this Polish frontier was deceptively peaceful— rolling grassy farmlands, gently rising mountains, cool forests and quiet villages with wayside shrines.

I had walked there among the same wild flowers we know back home: daisies, buttercups, dandelions, red clover and white, and Queen Anne's lace. Bees hummed in the apple orchards and at one point a brook sang in the no-man's land between the Czech and Polish frontier posts.

Seeing this border on a sleepy summer afternoon, it was hard to believe that at night this restful countryside was the setting for a nightmarish game of hide-and-seek between refugees and Polish frontier guards.

I had seen some of these guards and a bit of their handiwork on my visit to the border. In one Czech frontier village, the Czech and Polish border posts are less than one hundred feet apart. Between them was a white stucco farmhouse, with an elaborately carved wooden birdhouse perched high up beside it. There was a busy coming and going in the birdhouse, but the farmhouse stood deserted.

In the village I met the Czech who used to live in that house. He had a patch over his left eye and lifted the patch to show me an empty socket. The eye had been shot out by Polish border guards, who accused him of being a Czech spy. Since the shooting, he had moved out of his old home in that miniature but dangerous no-man's land and into the security of the village.

The Czech told me that he had lived in Breslau, then German Silesia, before the war. He had been an active anti-Fascist, had served a term in the prison at Breslau during the Hitler period, and been sent by the Nazis to Buchenwald for underground activity.

"You see that farmhouse up there," he said in German, pointing further up the frontier. "A Czech woman who lived there was murdered one night a few months ago. No one knows who killed her, but we all suspect it was done by Polish frontier guards."

I had bought a round of drinks for the Czech gendarmes in the village at a low-roofed tavern. They took me up to

the border but would not let me approach the frontier
gate until they had first spoken with the Polish guards on
the other side and handed out some American cigarettes
I had given them. I don't know why they took all these
precautions. I hardly thought they would shoot a man in
American uniform in broad daylight, no matter how close
I came to the border. But the Czech gendarmes wouldn't
let me walk up until they had established friendly contact.

The two Polish guards had walked across no-man's
land to get the cigarettes. They shook hands with me
across the barrier. In their makeshift uniforms, with knee
patches on their trousers and ill-matched jackets, they
looked like a pair of fierce *sans culottes* out of the French
Revolution. Both had rifles slung over their shoulders.
Conversation was limited, and my Czech friends and I
soon went back to the tavern for another round of the
local cherry brandy.

From the Czech gendarmes that afternoon and from
my comrades on the train late that night, I heard a good
deal about the difficulties and dangers encountered by
illegal emigrants on the Polish side of the frontier.

On the border, Jews attempting to leave Poland run a
double hazard. The first lies in the widespread anti-
Semitism which affects both the Polish peasantry along
the border and the border guards. The other lies in the
general lawlessness existing in the country: armed bandits
and underground Polish oppositionists who are both anti-
Semitic and opposed to the present government.

To get by the frontier posts and the border patrols
unseen is not easy, but a few refugees manage it, some-

times after many nights of watchful waiting in deep forest
and high-grassed meadow. One man on the train told me
he had come across the border with five other men and
two children. He said it took them five weeks of waiting
before they could find a way across without being seen
by the Polish guards.

Most refugees are caught on their way over. Occasionally they may find a Polish frontier guard who will let
them pass. More often they are stripped of all valuables
and any clothing of value before being allowed to proceed
to the more hospitable Czech side. Some remain on the
border in unmarked graves. There are few nights without
some shootings on the frontier.

The crossing is difficult enough for the men. It is a
fearful experience for the women and children. Some are
beaten by guards on the way over. There were several
bandaged heads on the train.

Sometimes a group of refugees finds a hidden route
across, or a frontier guard susceptible to bribery. One or
two of the braver may return to Poland to help other
groups over the frontier. A famous woman leader of the
Warsaw ghetto uprising made the return trip four or five
times in the region I visited, coming back each time with
another group of refugees until her activities became too
conspicuous, and she was forced to go on. She is now
living in Palestine.

From what the refugees told me it was apparent that
there were both a push and a pull across the border. The
push was out of Poland. The pull was toward Palestine.

There was a sturdy, broad-shouldered, jolly little Polish

Jew on the train, about five feet four. He was the only
other man except myself in the crowd with a complete
costume. Somehow, in the distribution of cast-off clothing
from America to refugees on the Czech side, he had fallen
heir to a green chauffeur's uniform in good condition. Its
neat lines and high collar gave him a military appearance
he had earned. For he had fought two years as a soldier
in the Red Army and then three years in the Polish Army.
He was a Polish Jew who was lucky enough to get across
the Russian border early in the war. He returned to his
native land as a soldier in the Polish Army and helped to
liberate Warsaw.

"And do you know the reception I got?" he asked me
in Yiddish. "I meet a Polish woman and she says to me
. . . I, who am a soldier in Polish uniform, mind you, and
she knew I was a Jew . . . to *me,* she said, 'The one bad
thing about Hitler is that he didn't kill all the Jews.' Do
you think I wanted to stay in Poland after that?"

My stalwart little friend's story was substantially the
same story I heard over and over again on the trip: Jews
returned from concentration camps in Germany or from
service in Russia; they very rarely located a relative or
friend alive; they found whole Jewish communities destroyed; and they felt themselves unwelcome, despised,
and hated in an atmosphere of virulent anti-Semitism.

"The Polish government is not anti-Semitic," I heard
over and over again, "but the Polish people are. The government's hold is weak. Conditions are lawless. Life is
dangerous. The government is trying its best to establish
new colonies and homes for the Jews, but the task is hope-

less. We have no future in Poland. We see only more pogroms ahead."

The "pull" toward Palestine I heard expressed again and again, not only from the young *khalutsim* on the train, but from older folk who would say, "I'm not a Zionist. I'm a Jew. That's enough. We have wandered enough. We have worked and struggled too long on the lands of other peoples. We must build a land of our own. *Mir muzen boyen a yiddish land.* [We must build a Jewish land.]"

There are few sights more depressing than one's first look at these Jews fleeing across the border. I had seen them earlier in the day in the Czech Red Cross hospital to which they are taken for a medical examination and clearance. The building had been a Hitler Youth hostel during the occupation. The smell from the basement latrines as we entered was overpowering. I got used to bad smells on the trip but I never encountered anything to match that first whiff in the hospital at Anton.

Through that thick and stinking atmosphere one came into a kitchen in which refugee women were preparing a one-dish meal of soup in two huge cauldrons. Beyond the kitchen was a dining room full of newly arrived refugees and a big room in which they were passing through their first medical examination.

They looked and smelled bad. Most of the men were undersized and underfed. The women were either scrawny or unhealthily obese, broad-beamed, and squat. The eyes of the children were the eyes of little people unpleasantly adult before their time. Men, women, and children, crowded together in that first reception center, ragged and unclean and tired, looked like the cast-offs of humanity.

The big news about the Jews of Eastern Europe is not that they have suffered. That is an old story, grown weary in the retelling. The real news is that so many of these people came across the border with tremendous vitality, with spirits unbroken.

Everywhere else in Europe I felt a defeatist spirit. In France again and again I heard it said *"France est fini"* [France is finished]. In Vienna young Austrians told me, "We are tired. The old Vienna will never come again. There is no future for Austria." In Italy one found the same weariness and hopelessness.

These Jews out of the East who have suffered more than any other people in the war in terms of sheer numbers slain, who returned to find themselves without home or family, have a will to live and a will to build that are wonderful to see.

I made many friends and *khaveyrim* on the long journey. I came to love these people among whom I traveled. And I understood why they broke into song as our train began to move out of Anton on a journey many of them would wait months, or forever, to complete.

III

The refugees I was with were lucky to be starting their underground trip to Palestine from the little town of

Anton on the Polish-Czech border. The story of Anton and its friendly attitude as I heard it on the train to Bratislava was, in large part, the story of two Czech Jews who lived there. I will call them Schweik and Hacek. Those were not their real names. These two, in their quiet, undramatic and hard-working way, were heroes of the illegal immigration. They had been willing to risk their high standing in their community and their friendly relations with their non-Jewish neighbors to help less fortunate Jews across the border and on their way to Palestine.

There were three hundred Jews before the war in this Czech town of twelve thousand. Only twenty survived. Schweik and Hacek were the first of the survivors to come home. Both came of old Czech-Jewish families. Schweik was a captain in the Czech Legion in the first World War, and became a successful manufacturer afterward. Hacek was also a local businessman. Both were sent to Auschwitz concentration camp by the Germans after the Czech occupation. One lost his parents and a brother; the other, his wife, child, and four sisters to the concentration camp and the crematorium.

Since their return, the government had restored not only their property but that of their dead relatives, and they had devoted their time and money to helping the illegal immigration.

I first heard of Schweik and Hacek in Prague from an underground worker to whom I had come along a kind of chain of command, and I went to see them as soon as I arrived in Anton. I located Schweik's office not far from the railroad station. The office was an oak-paneled affair

that would have done credit to an up-and-coming businessman in America. I showed underground credentials I carried in Hebrew. I told him I had heard of the work he and
his friend were doing, that I would like to see something of
it and then join the next illegal transport leaving the town
of Anton.

Schweik phoned Hacek to join us at lunch in Schweik's
home. Both were tall, fine-looking men, and both had concentration camp numbers tattooed on their arms.

Lunch in Schweik's old-fashioned three-story brick home
was served by an elderly Czech woman who had worked
for the family many years before the war. Schweik assured
me she spoke better Yiddish than he did. I found that
easy to believe since the Yiddish of the Czech Jews is
more German and Czech than Yiddish. This is the story
Schweik told me:

The infiltration of refugee Jews into the town of Anton
began during the revolution near the close of the war,
when the Czechs rose against the German occupation
authorities. There was a concentration camp for Jewish
women in the neighborhood and about five hundred and
sixty of these women were freed during the revolution and
went to Anton. They lived in makeshift emergency lodg-
ings for several weeks and then moved on into DP camps
in Germany.

Schweik and Hacek, as the first native Jews to return
to the town from concentration camp, did their best to
furnish food and lodging to other concentration camp survivors who went through the town on their way back to
their old homes.

"First," Schweik said, "people came through on their way back to Poland, but pretty soon a movement began in the opposite direction. Polish Jews began to return from Poland. They would tap on the windows in the middle of the night and ask for shelter. During the winter some came to us barefoot in the snow. The stories they told were much alike. They could find no trace of their families. The Polish government was not anti-Semitic, but the Polish people were. They preferred to return to the camps in Germany and wait for a chance to emigrate abroad to America or Palestine."

The work Schweik and Hacek did for these refugees had made them legendary figures among the Polish Jews. The "grapevine" had spread the fame of these two Czechs not only in Poland, but deep across the border into the Soviet Union. Sitting in that darkened dirty carriage, slowly making its way across the green Czechoslovakian countryside, I spoke with several Polish Jews from the USSR who had gone to Anton beccause of Schweik and Hacek.

"I first heard of them in Kazakstan," one Polish Jew told me. "I heard that the best place to cross the Polish-Czech border was at Anton, and that if one asked there for *Pan* Schweik or *Pan* Hacek one could be sure of a night's lodging and of help in making contact with the underground."

I gathered that at one time the popularity of Anton began to embarrass the local Czech authorities. About four months ago so many Jews had piled into the town that the authorities arrested some, but the result of that affair was only to further regularize the immigration.

Until that time Schweik and Hacek had carried the burden of the work unaided. This consisted, I gathered, not only in providing food, shelter, and transportation, but in facilitating passage over the border.

"I have good friends in America," Schweik said, with a smile, "who keep me plentifully supplied with American cigarettes. You can do a great deal in Europe today with a few cartons of American cigarettes."

Schweik and Hacek literally traded cigarettes for lives. They had friendly contacts with guards on both sides of the border, and a carton of cigarettes at the right spot often eased the way for a whole group of illegal emigrants.

At one time Schweik and Hacek appealed to UNRRA for aid and UNRRA sent an executive to the town, but he reported that there was no way under UNRRA regulations by which it could help. In December, 1945, the Joint Distribution Committee began to send Schweik and Hacek funds to cover the cost of food and tickets from Anton to Bratislava. And after the arrests the Czech Red Cross and the local authorities made a hospital available as a clearance and medical center for the "infiltrees."

Schweik and Hacek told me that five thousand Jews had come across the border through their town during the preceding twelve months. Between May 1 and June 4 alone there were 1,530 immigrants. The day before I got there, one hundred and forty-eight crossed the border and the day I was there fifty-one came over. They told me they expected a hundred or more the next day. I didn't ask how

they knew this. One does not ask too many questions on
the underground route.

Over the border in this area came Czechs and Germans
as well as Jews, and some odd characters occasionally
turned up. One time eight German SS men were discovered
among the Jewish refugees. A Czech doctor supervising
medical examinations saw the tattoo marks all SS men
bear under their armpits, and turned them over to the
Czech police.

There were two kinds of Jewish refugees coming across
the Czech border. One was made up of Polish Jews who
had returned from German concentration camps only to
find life intolerable in their old homes. The other consisted of those Polish Jews who had fled into Russia after
the war began or lived in the eastern territories annexed
by the Soviet Union under the Ribbentrop-Molotov pact.
Those who wished to return did so legally under the Russo-
Polish repatriation agreement.

There was one striking difference between these Jews
from Russia and those pouring into the underground from
the European countries which were under Nazi domination
or influence. Out of the Soviet Union alone came the miracle of whole Jewish families. Only among these refugees
did one see fathers and mothers with children.

I heard of no Polish Jews coming out of Russia because
they wanted to live in Poland. All those I talked with—
and I encountered many on the underground route—left
with the intention of making their way out of Poland.
Most of them wanted to go to Palestine. Their favorite
exit route seemed to be to take trains in Poland for the new

areas of Jewish resettlement in the Silesian areas annexed by Poland and then to jump the train and head for the Czech border. This was not as easy as it sounds. Perhaps one in a hundred succeeded in getting across. There were some eighty thousand Jews waiting in the Silesian territory for a chance to get out of Poland.

Many of the Jews coming out of Russia had covered incredible distances. Jews from as far away as Vladivostok had crossed in the region I visited. One Polish Jewish physician with his whole family, including his seventy-five-year-old father, came through from Tibet; the physician had a brother who was president of the Joint Distribution Committee Fund in Venezuela. It took this physician and his family four months to reach Moscow from Tibet. Three days before my visit, one repatriated refugee from a small town four thousand meters east of Irkutsk crossed the border with ten children.

Western Czechoslovakia was a favorite crossing place for the illegal immigration. By western Czechoslovakia I mean Bohemia and Moravia, the Czech lands, for Czechoslovakia was a house divided between the democratic and cultured Czech country in the west, and backward peasant Slovakia in the east. Nowhere in eastern and central Europe were Jewish refugees more humanely treated than in the Czech provinces. But Slovakia, in this as in other respects, was a different story. Slovakia was an "independent" state under the Nazis and collaborated with them. It was a backward region culturally, under reactionary clerical influence, a festering place of Fascism and anti-Semitism. It was far easier for Jewish refugees to cross the Czech border, though they managed to get across the Slovak one, too.

The refugees I was traveling with all wondered what would be our own reception on Slovak soil. What would happen when we got to Bratislava, the capital of Slovakia?

"Do you think they'd dare to try and send us back," one youthful *khaluts* asked me, "or will we be able to go on from there to Vienna?"

IV

We were not the only travelers of our kind in the wake of World War II. At way stations and on the sidings to which we were shunted to let more important trains pass, we saw other trains loaded with refugees. In ancient third-class carriages like ours we saw Poles going east, and in battered freight cars *Volksdeutsche* going west. It was easy to recognize freight cars carrying refugee cargo. They were almost always crudely decorated with branches and fresh green leaves.

The *Volksdeutsche* were a special kind of Germans, the creation of the Nazi regime. Among those we passed were Polish citizens of German ancestry, never too welcome in the old Poland, who had enjoyed a brief period as *Herren-volk* during the Nazi occupation. Officially they were being repatriated. Actually they were being expelled by the Poland they had betrayed. They were bound for a Germany some of them had never seen. I had encountered some of

these *Volksdeutsche* in the Reich on my way to Czechoslovakia, and I knew that now that Germany had been defeated they were returning with resentment and anxiety.
There would be no joy of homecoming for them. I never
heard the *Volksdeutsche* sing.

I never heard singing from the Polish cars either. Some
of the returning Poles were ex-prisoners of war, but most
of them, like the Polish Jews with whom I was traveling,
had been in German concentration camps. They were
going home like the *Volksdeutsche,* in apprehension. The
DP camps from which they had come were largely under
the control of anti-Government Poles, drawn from the
Anders' Army. Even when these camp officials advised
their people to go home, the advice was hardly couched
in encouraging terms.

I heard of one Polish aristocrat who went back to Poland
secretly and illegally to see for himself before deciding
what to tell the displaced Poles under his care.

"Go back to Poland," he told his people when he returned. "Most of you were peasants, as were your fathers
before you. You knew nothing of politics before and you
know nothing of politics now. The land you tilled is still
there, and it must be tilled again, whatever the régime.
That is your place. Go back to it."

But he did not go back with them.

Sometimes our train and the trains carrying the other
refugees stopped on opposite sides of the same platform,
and people from both got out to stretch their legs. But
there was no mixing. No one shouted across the platform
from one train to the other. Their mutual misery created

no common bond between peoples who regarded each other as oppressors and oppressed. The hate and fear that flowed between us was almost tangible, like a thick current in the hot summer night.

"They have one advantage over us," an elderly Jew with a beard said to me in Yiddish, during one of these encounters. "They at least have a country of their own."

Our homelessness was reflected in the squeamish terminology applied to Jewish refugees. We were DP's—displaced persons. The term itself, for victims of Hitlerism, was a model of detached and frigid understatement. Some of us were Polish Jews repatriated from the Soviet Union, but others were Polish-Jewish DP's who were coming back from Poland—where the "displaced" had presumably been "replaced"—to the DP camps in the American zone of Germany and Austria.

For these people, official parlance had created a new category and a new euphemism: "Unsuccessful repatriatees." Even the shameful illegality of our border crossings had been covered with a custom-made, polysyllabic and refined little fig-leaf. We were "infiltrees." But nowhere in the records were my comrades referred to simply as Jews, although it was as Jews that they had suffered, and it was as Jews that most of them wanted a chance to live.

There wasn't too much food on the train. At the Red Cross hospital, on the Polish-Czech border, each of the refugees had been given a large loaf of dark rye bread for the trip to Bratislava. In their rucksacks and bags, buried in their few bits of clothing, many had hidden a jar of jam or a bit of sausage or cheese. A few had acquired, somewhere, somehow, small cans of sardines. A good many had a clove of garlic to rub on the bread and a bit of salt. Those men on the train who carried jack-knives passed them around to cut the bread, but many people just broke off pieces to eat. They ate heartily. On my underground trip I was to learn what a good meal could be made of dark brown bread with garlic rubbed over it, and salt.

I had a special treat for the comrades with whom I traveled. All they had to eat was bread, but I had come well prepared. I had gone shopping in Anton in preparation for the trip. I bought a kilo [two and two-tenths pounds] of sausage, a half dozen large white rolls, and a pound of assorted pastry. We had a grand meal together. The eyes of the *khalutsim* lit up when they saw the sausage. The white rolls were as great a delicacy.

At first they politely declined both the sausage and the white rolls.

"That's your supper," they said. "We have plenty to eat."

But, after a little coaxing, they succumbed to the smell of the sausage, and pretty soon we had everything divided up evenly as befits comrades.

I provided dessert for everybody in the car. I had brought several pounds of caramels from America. I gave everybody in the car, including the Czech secret service officer, a caramel. But for the *khalutsim* I had a special treat: an unopened box of American chocolates, bought in the Army's PX at Nuremberg on my way to Czechoslovakia. The chocolates were good. Like all normal youngsters the *khalutsim* had a "sweet tooth."

"Do you know," said one of the girls, "this is the first chocolate I've tasted in six years?"

My popularity was firmly established.

The oddest person I met on the train was a twenty-one-year-old *Chassid* whose name was Lain Sholem. The *Chassidim* are a mystical religious sect who revolted against the arid formalistic ritualism of orthodox Judaism. Sholem had a thin fringe of beard, small gold-rimmed spectacles and an old man's manner.

Sholem told me he was born near Smolensk in 1925. He attended the Russian schools but after school studied with his father, who was a *Chassidic* rabbi. He worked at his trade of bookbinder in Gorki during the war and came out of Russia under the Russo-Polish repatriation agreement as the husband of a Polish wife. The wife wasn't on the train, and I suspect it was a marriage of convenience to get him out of the Soviet Union.

I asked Sholem where he wanted to go.

"*Ergets tsu trakhten* [Somewhere I can think]," he said.

"Do you want to go to Palestine or America?" I asked. He said it didn't matter to him.

"What do you want to be?" was my next question.

"A *shoykhet* [a kosher slaughterer]" was the answer.

It was strange to see this youngster who had been born in the middle of one of the great revolutions of world history and apparently had been untouched by it. He had the mannerism of an old-fashioned East European rabbi. When I asked a question, he would cup one hand behind his ear, though he was not deaf, and say: "*Ha, vos zogt ir, hah?*"

[What are you saying, hah?]" I asked Sholem what he thought of the Soviet Union. The look in his little eyes was that of a man who considers himself too clever to be tripped up by such dangerous questions.

"Of that," he said, "I would rather say nothing."

Ours was a long and slow journey. We stopped not only at every one-tank town, but often on sidings along the way to let faster trains pass. At 7:10 p.m. we changed trains at a town called Chocen.

In Czechoslovakia, there are many outdoor cafés on railroad station platforms. There was a very attractive one at Chocen, with gay cloths on the tables.

When our train stopped at the station, the well-dressed folk eating dinner at the station café looked up in startled surprise to see the rabble emerging from that last car and swarming across the tracks to the train for Bratislava.

On the new train we also had the last car, another third-class carriage very much like the first, and there my *khaluts* friends, the man with the mandolin, and I again found a compartment to ourselves.

V

The youngest of the ten *khalutsim* had the usual story to tell. The usual story on the Jewish underground in Europe was a story of suffering, tragedy, and melodramatic escape from wholesale murder. But his had an unexpectedly happy ending that gave a vicarious thrill to every one of us in that third-class railroad car crowded with refugees.

He was sixteen. I had noticed him first when I had boarded the train at Anton. Six years of danger and under-feeding hadn't helped his growth and he was about as tall as a boy of twelve. But he had an attractive fun-loving small boy's glint in his eye. Somewhere along the way he had lost four front teeth, and his jaw was bandaged. I never found out why. His name was Abram Wroclawski and he came from Lodz in Poland.

His comrades called him Avrumikel and Avrumele— diminutives for Abram—and he was obviously the "baby" and the pet of the group. We had plenty of time to talk on that all-night journey. I sat next to him in the hard-seat compartment I shared with the *khalutsim.* I asked him where he came from and how he had managed to survive.

"I was only nine when the war came," Avrumikel told me in Yiddish. "I was a student in a Polish school. There were two hundred thousand Jews in Lodz. The Germans put us all into a ghetto and closed it up. There were seven in my family, my father and mother, two sisters, and three brothers. It was very hard to get food in the ghetto and many people died of hunger. My father died in 1942, my mother a few months later. My two older brothers died in the ghetto in 1943.

"In 1944, the Nazis liquidated the ghetto and trans-ferred those of us who were still alive to the concentra-tion camp at Auschwitz. I had a sister who was then twelve years old. *Zey hoben ir geshikt farbrent tsu veren* [They

—meaning the Germans—sent her to be burned; i.e., the gas chamber and the crematorium]."

"I was also in a group which was to be sent to the crematorium. We all suspected what was in store for us, and when we came to the death wagons which were to take us to the crematorium, I ran away. I knew I had nothing to lose and that the worst that could happen to me was to be shot as I fled. Somehow I managed to get away in the excitement. I suppose my small size was a help.

"I fled seven kilometers to Babitz, hiding in the fields and forests by day and moving by night. I was in a tough spot because the only clothes I had were my *KZ* pajamas. There was no chance of getting away in those and I did not know how to get other clothes. So I had to go to another concentration camp.

"I slipped into the camp at night. There were Poles and Jews there and German political prisoners. A German communist in the camp took a liking to me. I was sick and starved and had to be kept hidden from the guards. He brought me food and saved my life.

"I couldn't be kept hidden forever. My friend went to a Jewish inmate who worked in the SS bureau at the camp. Through this Jew I obtained papers as a prisoner. There were hundreds in the camp and as long as I had these papers I could move about freely. I was just one more Jewish prisoner. I stayed there four months and was then transferred to Buchenwald.

"I spent the rest of war in Buchenwald. We worked in nearby factories by day, usually twelve hours or more, with little to eat. Many of us died of hunger. Three days before the Americans arrived, the SS guards took forty thousand Jews out of the camp. The Jews were told that they were being transferred but those of us who were lucky enough to be left in the camp later learned that they had been taken to prepared graves in a forest not far away and shot.

"The day after that, there were rumors that the American troops were only ten kilometers away and our SS guards fled. On April 11, 1945, *halb fir* [at 3:30] I was set free. Those of us who were strong enough cheered and wept with joy. The Americans were very good to us, but some prisoners were so weak from long starvation that the liberation came too late.

"I stayed in Buchenwald two months after the liberation. I knew my father, mother, two brothers, and one sister were dead, but I thought that perhaps the other sister might still be alive. As soon as I felt strong enough to travel I wanted to go search for her. Just before the Russians took over that territory, an American officer told me I could get home on an UNRRA repatriation train to look for her. When I got back to Lodz I found her. There she is."

Avrumikel pointed to a girl who had been listening to his story with a smile. All the *khalutsim* turned to me expectantly, to see if I shared their happy feeling. Among the refugees who had been in concentration camps, few ever found even distant relatives. To have returned home and discovered a sister was little less than a miracle. Now brother and sister were going together to Palestine.

The sister was nineteen, with bright blue eyes and dark curly hair. She was not much taller than her brother. Her name was Sarah. She too had been sent to Auschwitz from the Lodz ghetto.

"I said good-by to my little sister there and to my other friends," Sarah said, "for we all expected to be sent to the crematorium. But I was strong and old enough to work so the Germans sent me instead to Magdeburg.

"I finally went to Bergen-Belsen concentration camp. We were put to work in a German munitions factory. I was at a machine that smoothed the cases for bullets. I found it very hard to work. I would stand at the machine and cry so much that I couldn't see through my tears. I thought 'these bullets are killing the people I love' and I would cry harder.

"One day a woman foreman, a German, came to me and asked why I cried. I told her, and she showed me how without attracting attention I could spoil the bullets so they would not shoot. After that I stopped crying.

"We worked very hard on little more than thin soup and bread. It seemed that we worked day and night, march-ing back and forth in the darkness and cold to the con-centration camp for a few hours sleep each day. Many could stand no more and just lay down and died. It seemed an endless agony, through which we passed half asleep.

"When the American troops broke into Germany and began to approach Bergen-Belsen, the German guards took us out of the camp. They said they were transferring us to another camp further in the interior. They said the Americans might shoot us. We knew that was a lie.

"When we stopped for our first rest on the road, the Germans began shooting at us from all sides. Some of us

had fallen asleep alongside the road. Others just sat too
weary to sleep. Many were shot running away. I was one
of the lucky few who escaped.

"I got to Loburg, about forty kilometers from Magdeburg. There, on the 8th of May, 1945, I was freed by the
Russians, and *ikh hob balt gefort aheym* [and I at once
started traveling home]."

I asked Sarah how she traveled back to Poland and she
said she made the trip on foot.

"It was quite a journey," she said with a wry smile.
"There were hundreds of us on the roads, making for home.

"But when I got back to Lodz I found I had no home.
The house we lived in had been burned to the ground. I
could not find even distant relatives and I saw only one or
two of my old friends. Most of the Poles I encountered
hated the Jews more than ever.

"Then," Sarah said, "*hob ikh gezeyn az fur yiden is
nit tu kayn ander veg* [I saw that for Jews there was
no other way left open] and I entered a *kibbutz* and
began to prepare myself for Palestine."

Sarah said she had not been a Zionist before the war.
She entered the *kibbutz* at *Dror*. She learned Hebrew and
tailoring, and it was there that her brother found her. Her
brother also joined the colony. He picked chauffeuring for
his trade.

"Our trade school," her brother said, "had one jeep
an American soldier had given us and we all practiced
on that."

The two children told me they lost one uncle in the

Warsaw ghetto and had another uncle in the Warsaw ghetto and another in New York.

"I haven't written to him," Avrumikel said, "but I'd like him to know we are on our way to *Eretz Israel* [Palestine]."

I telephoned the news to his uncle in New York when I got back.

VI

Many of the Jews who survived the Hitler period were people who passed as Aryans. There was one such person among us. She was a short, stocky blonde of twenty from Lwow, which was Polish before the war and is part of the Soviet Ukraine today. Her name was Sarah Barach and one would have taken her for a Slavic *shikse* [gentile girl] of Polish or Ukrainian origin. This had been her salvation.

Under the German occupation, Sarah had lived in a ghetto in Lwow. When the ghetto was liquidated, Sarah and her mother were among those loaded on the death wagons bound for the gas chamber and the crematorium. Sarah jumped off the wagon along the way and escaped in the darkness after one last quick hug and kiss from her mother. The guards didn't see her, and her Aryan appearance made it easy for her to find shelter and work.

Life as an Aryan also had its hazards in that part of the

world. Lwow is Polish, but the countryside is Ukrainian. Before the war the Roman Catholic Poles treated the Uniat and Orthodox Ukrainians worse than they did the Jews. The Nazis did their best during the occupation to fan the old hatred between the Poles and the Ukrainians.

"I lived as a Pole," Sarah told me, "working as a servant girl and farmhand in the country until, late in 1942, Ukrainians began murdering Poles. I had to flee, but when I settled down again on a farm to work I said I was a Ukrainian and it was as a Ukrainian that I lived until the Russians reconquered that territory. I spoke both Polish and Ukrainian fluently.

"The only narrow escape I had was the result of a dream. I dreamed I was home with my mother. The next morning the wife of the peasant for whom I worked said: 'I heard you singing a Jewish song in your sleep last night.' I was frightened, but laughed it off. I said it was a song I had learned when I worked as a servant girl for Jews before the war."

Sarah had an odd story to tell when I asked her whether she had come across any Germans friendly to the Jews.

"While working as a Ukrainian, I once met a *Wehrmacht* soldier," Sarah related. "In the course of our conversation, I said to him in broken German: 'Those Jews are no good.' His answer surprised me."

" 'Some Jews are no good,' the German soldier replied. 'But I have known some very good Jews.' And then he added a surprising sentence. He spoke simply, as to a person who didn't understand his language well. 'Hitler no good,' the Wehrmacht soldier told me. He said it like a person who had stored that thought up a long time, and was both relieved and frightened to get it off his chest."

Four of the *khalutsim* were Polish Jews who had known life under both the Russians and the Germans. Dov Potashnick, a nineteen-year-old boy from a little Jewish town called Oszmiana near Vilna, was pointed out to me as the author of the song I heard when I first boarded the refugee train for Bratislava, *"Khalutsim, Greyten Zikh Far Eretz Israel."* His home town was occupied by the Russians after the invasion of Poland in 1939. I asked him how he found it under the Russians.

"Gants gut, nit shlekht [Quite good, not at all bad]," was his answer. "But in 1941 the Germans came and then our *tsores* [sorrow] began. In a week we were all wearing yellow *Mogen Dovids* [six-pointed Jewish stars] on our arms. A month later I lost my father and elder brother when the SS surrounded our town and shot eight hundred men.

"The rest of us were put into a ghetto where I lived with my mother and sister until 1943. In 1943 the ghetto was liquidated. The last I saw of my mother and sister was when they were taken away with other women to Auschwitz, where they were gassed and burned. I was sent to a camp in Stutthoff, later to Buchenwald and then to Rhinesdorf. We were slave workers and I was one of the lucky few who survived the endless work and meager food.

"In April, 1945, with the American troops only thirty kilometers away, the Germans began to move us to a new camp in Czechoslovakia. We traveled for five days in slow freight trains, with nothing to eat but a few potatoes. On the way the train was bombed and we ran away, but the SS men recaptured about one thousand of us and marched us off on foot to Theresienstadt in Czechoslovakia. Those who couldn't stand the march were shot. Eight hundred of us arrived. I, like many others, was feverish and spotted with typhus. There, a few days later, on May 9, 1945, we were freed. I was sick for several months and then went back to Lodz, where I entered a *kibbutz* to prepare myself for life as a pioneer in Palestine."

I told Potashnick that getting to Palestine wouldn't be quite as easy as boarding a train to Bratislava, that he might have to wait months in a DP camp in Germany before he could start for Palestine, and then run a British blockade to enter.

"I'll get there," Potashnick said confidently. "Those are minor troubles after the things I've been through."

Myra Bergman, a sandy-haired slim girl of twenty-five who came from Thorn in Poland, was one of the lucky few who escaped from the German-occupied zone into the Soviet Union.

"Shortly after the Germans occupied Poland in 1939," Myra related, "all the Jews in my town were summoned to gather in the *plats* [the central square]. There were six thousand of us. It was a cold, wintry evening. We were marched off on foot without baggage to Warsaw.

"During the night some of us managed to slip away. I made for the new Russian frontier [the Ribbentrop-Molotov line]. A German soldier captured me on the

border and cursed me. 'You must be a communist,' he
shouted, 'if you're trying to get into the Soviet Union.'
But when I cried and pleaded with him, he let me go
over the border.

"But that was not the end of my troubles. There was
a no-man's land between the German and Russian borders.
I had got over the German border, but now couldn't cross
the Russian. The Russians wouldn't let us in. There were
several thousand Jews in that area. The snows had begun
and it was bitterly cold. We had no shelter. Peasants
smuggled food into the area, but at prices few could af-
ford to pay. It cost ten *zlotys* [about $1.80] for a liter
of milk.

"We were there eight days. Finally, in desperation, we
stormed the Russian border, overpowered the guards and
got across. We made our way to Byalostok, about sixty
miles from the Ribbentrop-Molotov line. There we got
help from the Jewish community.

"Shortly after we arrived," Myra said, "the Russian
Government ordered the evacuation of Jewish and other
refugees from that border region to the interior of the
Soviet Union. The Russians were already preparing for a
possible German attack. We were in the first defense zone.
It is fortunate for us, though we did not know it at the
time, that we were moved. Twenty thousand of us were
transported on sleighs to various *kolkhozes* [collective
farms] in Russia and the Ukraine."

I asked Myra how Jewish refugees were treated in the
collective settlements.

"Zeyr gut oyfgenemen [Very well received]" was

her answer. "At the *kolkhoz* to which I was sent, we were greeted with a parade and a band as victims of Fascism. The people there were *zeyr moralishe mentshen* [very moral people]. We worked hard on the farm and learned manual trades."

Myra added a significant sentence about her experience before the German attack in 1941. Myra said that she and the other refugees at that *kolkhoz* had *"gornit gefilt zikh yiden* [had not at all felt themselves Jews]," but had been made to feel at home and in no way different from the other people in the collective.

"When the Germans attacked," Myra went on, "we were again evacuated, this time to Tashkent in Asiatic Russia, north of Afghanistan. It was a terrible journey. Transport was disorganized. We had little bread to eat. Typhus broke out on the way, but we were well treated on our arrival. We worked on farms in Uzbekistan during the war, and after the war was over I went back to Poland to see if I could find any relatives. I found none.

"The reception we got in Poland was not a pleasant one. The first thing we heard when the repatriates came across the Polish border from the USSR were cries of *"zhidi kommunisti"* [Jew Communists]. For those Poles we were only more Jews to kill. I don't ever want to see Poland again."

VII

I don't think I shall ever forget that first night on the train to Bratislava. There were no lights. Imagine a darkened third-class compartment for eight in which there were twelve of us: the ten *khalutsim,* the man with the mandolin, and myself.

We halted every fifteen or twenty minutes at stations or on sidings. Once, just before midnight, we stopped at a station with a lunch stand and I bought big sugared cookies for the children—the *khalutsim,* none of them more than in their early twenties, seemed children to me, no different from my own three at home.

It was a starry night, cool and clear, and one's eyes grew accustomed to the darkness. Outside one saw what seemed an endless procession of sleeping Czech and later Slovak farmhouses, hamlets, and small towns. The old-fashioned yellow lamps at the stations and the crossroads threw their light into the compartment as we passed them.

The man with the mandolin played and one *khaveyr* [comrade] after another sang. I have never heard singing that touched me so much. The songs I heard were songs that had sprung from the Nazi-created ghettoes, the concentration camps, and the forest hideouts of the Jewish Partisan bands. Many were the spontaneous creation of anonymous longing.

One of the songs I heard was a *Volkslied* [a people's

song] about a small East European village called Slutsk.
Before Hitler, there were many such Jewish villages in
Poland and the Ukraine. The song evoked memories of a
Jewish life which has passed away forever. Except for a
scattered remnant, the pious Jews who lived in those vil-
lages are dead.

The refrain of the song was *"Slutsk, mayn Slutsk, mayn
shtetl, ikh benk nokh dir"* [Slutsk, my Slutsk, my little
hometown, I long for you]. There were lines in it that
provided vivid glimpses of the life of young *khalutsim*
on the train had known as children and would never see
again. One stanza pictured the village on *erev shabes*
[Sabbath eve, Friday night] when the Sabbath candles
were lit and there were prayer services in the synagogue.
I remember two lines:

> *Fleygt di Mama bentshen*
> *Tate fleygt in Beth Hamidrash geyn*
> [Mother used to bless the Sabbath candles,
> Father used to go to *Beth Hamidrash*]

The *Beth Hamidrash,* the social center of an orthodox
village, was a house used during the week for the study
of the *Torah* [Bible and Law] and for worship on holi-
days and the Sabbath.

To hear the song was to see the village peaceful with
the new Sabbath, to see the white linen and the fresh
baked *challah* [white twisted bread] on the table, mother
saying her Sabbath prayers over the newly lit candles in
the brass seven-pronged *Menorah.* Father would be washed
and in his Sabbath best, going off with his cronies to the
Beth Hamidrash. If I, who had never known that life,

could see it as I heard the singing, imagine how vivid it must have been to those who had lived it as children and were now leaving it forever!

The sixteen-year-old "baby" of the *khalutsim*, Avru-mikel, sang another ghetto song about a Jewish town. The song is called *"Es brent"* and it pictures a village being burned by the Nazis: *"Es brent, bruderle, es brent"* [It is burning, little brother, it is burning]. I remember one line. It went, *"Lesht mit ayer aygen blut"* [Extinguish it with your own blood].

Another song, *"In Sahara,"* told of a dream in which one found oneself in a land of palaces with silver doors and gardens with trees from which the birds sang. The dreamer awakens in the concentration camp. The chorus was:

Es iz a ligen
Es iz a ligen
Es iz a puster troym
Der midber iz keyn land, keyn feld un keyn boym.
[It is a lie
It is a lie
It is a futile dream
In the desert is no land, no field and no tree.]

I heard a *lager lid* [concentration camp song] called "Treblinka." Treblinka was the name of a concentration camp. "We used to sing it at night as we lay in the con-centration camp," Avrumikel told me. "It was comforting to sing." The song is a song of lost homes and parents with a chorus which goes:

Treblinka dort
Far yeden yid der gute ort

Ver's kumt ahin
Farblaybt shoyn dort
Dort in Treblinka.
[Treblinka there
For every Jew the 'Good Place'
Who comes there
Remains there always
There in Treblinka.]
"Good Place" is Yiddish idiom for cemetery.

One ghetto song called "In a Lithuanian Village" told the story of a little girl whose mother places her in a Christian orphan asylum to save her life. (On the illegal boat to Palestine I was later to meet a girl of ten whose life was saved in just this way.) The child pleads with her mother, *"Ikh vil mama geyn mit dir . . . ikh vil nit blayben do aleyn"* [I want to go with you, Mother, I don't want to stay here alone].

The mother kisses and comforts her, but tells the child the orphanage must be her home if her life is to be saved. The mother sings to the child that from then on the child will never again hear:

Keyn yiddish vort,
Keyn yiddish lid,
Fun haynt, mayn kind,
Bist mer keyn yid.
[No Jewish word,
No Jewish song,
From today on, my child,
You are no more a Jew.]
The child pleads but the mother pushes her into the

orphanage and runs into the street *"mit royte oygen fin geveyn"* [her eyes red with tears] and she explains in the song that like the mother of Moses she had no recourse but to put her child in strange hands, *"andersh hob ikh nit gekent"* [I could not do otherwise].

This is a very sentimental song. It is one thing to read in cold print, it was another to hear it sung by a girl *khaluts* who had herself lost her mother, to hear it in a darkened train compartment rumbling across the Czecho-slovak plains, in a car filled with refugees.

For these children, on their way out of Europe, the songs they sang said farewell to vanished homes and parents. Every once in a while one of the *khalutsim* would retreat into the shadows and I would see a head bend and shoulders shake. The girls mothered each other, and the *khalutsim* slept leaning one against the other.

Toward three in the morning, with everyone asleep, I stepped carefully over their feet and went to the back of the car. I stood watching the rails stretch out behind us in the darkness until the sky began to grow gray with the first hints of dawn.

Through the Iron Curtain

I

We reached Bratislava at 5:30 the morning after leaving Anton. It was a cold dawn and Bratislava, with its onion-shaped church towers and massive stone buildings, looked grayer than usual under that sunless sky.

The Czech secret service officer in plain clothes who was our guard and escort helped the women shoulder their bags and knapsacks as the train came into the station. We must have made an odd spectacle as we trooped out of the station and straggled down the street.

We were a sleepy-looking, unshaven, unwashed, and

ragged horde led along the streets by a sheepish-looking elderly Czech gentleman. One little boy was marching briskly along in his bare feet, his precious one pair of shoes slung over his shoulders. Near him walked the skinniest little woman I have ever seen: she looked like the pictures of people who had been starved almost to death in concentration camps. She had on only a thin dress, and shivered with cold and fatigue.

Two women carried babies. A short man strode along in a big Russian army overcoat that was meant for a much larger fellow. It fell below his ankles and sagged over his narrow shoulders. The *khalutsim* looked drowsy and a little resentful, like children who have just been told that it's time to get up and go to school.

There were few carts or people on the streets. The first sign of color and activity was encountered when we came to newly renamed Stalinova Square.

The big square was full of peasants who had come into town with their wagons to sell their produce. They had set up makeshift stands on which were piled red cherries, white radishes, green peppers, yellow onions, fresh white cheeses, and flowers of many kinds.

On one side of the square was a melancholy looking iron-colored old church with a bulbous Byzantine tower. On the other lay our destination, the Hotel Jelen, the UNRRA repatriation center in Bratislava.

The hotel was a medieval, stone building which might once have been the town house and fastness of a Slovak nobleman. It had long passed its time of glory. The few windows in front were encrusted with dirt. It had been bombed by the Russians and a hole gaped on one side of the roof.

We went through a small door which had been cut in what was formerly a wooden entrance large enough to admit a nobleman's four-in-hand. On the right was the UNRRA office, where we awakened an elderly and querulous concierge who had been sleeping in his clothes.

In front of us, beyond the arched entrance, was a large courtyard circled by a broken balcony of iron grillwork. There was horse dung in the court. Obviously it hadn't been swept for days.

An ancient staircase of stone curved upward in a magnificent spiral just inside the grand entrance, but the steps were chipped and broken. An old mirror on the stairs mocked us with our own ragged images as we mounted to the reception room on the next floor.

We left our bags in a big room that contained a few rickety single beds and many cot mattresses on the floor. The place was filthy. The interior was bomb damaged; water had leaked in, adding one more hue to the discoloration of the unpapered walls.

The stairway walls were scrawled over with handwriting. One saw this kind of scrawl in every reception center in Europe and along the stairs in every building housing a Jewish organization. Refugees wrote their names and home towns on every wall they came to with the hope that some friend or relative might see them. Our refugees, having rid themselves of their baggage, went immediately to read the names, each trying to find someone he used to know, or perhaps a relative.

Even those who knew they had no one left joined with
the others in reading along the walls—just in case; who
knows? The age of miracles had not yet passed. And anyway it was thrilling to be there when a familiar name was
discovered. None of our group found any names that
morning.

A harassed young Jewish attendant insisted that the
Czech officer and I come up to his private apartment on
the third floor. It was a single room with a washstand
behind a screen, a wooden table with three chairs, and
an unmade cot on which he slept. We were to have breakfast with him, he said, and when he went out to shop I
went downstairs to say good-by to the *khalutsim*. They
were to have their breakfast at a Joint Distribution Committee canteen.

We breakfasted on white radishes, sour cream, rye
bread with butter and hot coffee. The Czech seemed as
moved by what he had seen and heard on the trip from
Anton as I was. When he left I thanked him for the kindness he had shown the refugees.

My next stop was to be Vienna. But I did not yet know
how I or my refugee comrades would succeed in making
that second leg of our journey.

II

The Jewish underground representative in Bratislava
did his best to dissuade me from traveling the illegal route
through the Russian zone of Austria to Vienna.

I had gone to the Hotel Carlton. I wanted a hot bath and a little time alone. I had just finished dressing and was looking out the casement window over the Balkan rooftops to the Danube when there was a knock on my door.

My visitor was a young *sheliakh.* His name was Isak, and he had been sent to Bratislava because he was of Slovak birth, spoke the language fluently and knew the country well. He was in his late twenties, dark eyed, with a touch of swarthiness in his skin. He looked Hungarian as do many of the Slovak Jews.

His name was on my list of underground contacts and I showed him my underground passport.

I asked how I could get to Vienna. I had a military transit visa for the French and American zones in Austria from the American military attaché in Prague, but had no clearance for the Soviet zone. Isak thought I should get an Austrian visa and take the bus to Vienna, where I could rejoin the refugees at the Rothschild Memorial Hospital. I told him I preferred to go by the illegal route.

"You'll be very uncomfortable," he said, "and you'll have to walk eight kilometers [about five miles] across the border. Why don't you take the bus and see these people again in Vienna?"

I told him I didn't mind being uncomfortable and that I didn't mind walking. I asked if he was thinking only of my comfort or if he was afraid that my presence in the illegal convoy might make trouble. I said that I didn't want to endanger the crossing but that if I would cause no embarrassment I wanted to go along.

Isak assured me he was thinking only of my comfort
and that if I really wanted to travel the illegal route I was
welcome. We decided it would be better, however, if I
went in civilian clothes as a refugee lest the correspondent's uniform create suspicion in the Russian zone. It was
arranged for me to turn up at the Hotel Jelen at one
o'clock the next afternoon for the trip across the border.

After lunch I shopped. Bratislava was one of the few
places in Europe where food was plentiful and unrationed.
This was so even during the war when Slovakia was an
"independent" state under the Nazis. The Germans used
to vacation there. They called it "Schweinland," either
because pork was plentiful or as a reflection on the country
itself. I bought two kilos of salami and some candy to feed
my *khaluts* comrades on the way to Vienna. They did not
expect to see me again and I looked forward to surprising
them.

Two kinds of refugees get through to Bratislava. One
comes in a more or less regular way from points on the
Czech-Polish border, as I had. Others cross the Slovak
border from Poland and make their way to Bratislava as
best they can.

My first morning in Bratislava I encountered six
khalutsim, three boys and three girls, who had reached
Bratislava without aid of any sort. I found them on the
stairs of a Jewish organization which had not yet opened
for the day. One of the girls was lying on the steps crying.

I offered her some chocolate which she tearfully refused. I asked one of the others what was the matter. He
told me their group had come across the Tatra mountains

from Poland into Slovakia, that the girl was crying from weariness but would be all right once she had a chance to rest.

To come over the Tatras is a difficult and hazardous journey. Hiding out in those mountains were SS men, remnants of the Anders' anti-government Polish forces and renegade Red Army soldiers who had served under the turncoat Russian General Bender. They seemed to have a plentiful supply of dollars and pounds, which they spent in the villages on either side of the border.

One of the *khalutsim* was wearing a Red army uniform and boots. His name was Schmulik Segal. He came from Grovno in what was then Poland, and had been a lieutenant in the Red Army. He said he had fought his way west with the army from Stalingrad to Lwow and then on to Vienna. He was wounded, spent four and a half months in a hospital in the Caucasus and then fought in the Russian campaign against Japan.

"When the war against Japan ended I went to Khaborovsk," Schmulik told me, "and was sent back to Moscow, where I was demobilized and given my papers back to Poland as a Polish citizen. I found no one I knew in Poland, except my brother Yankel who fought in the Polish Army. Our old home was destroyed and we entered a collective to train for Palestine."

Sometimes these unescorted tours across Slovakia did not end so well. I was packing at the hotel later that same morning when Isak arrived, very much disturbed. He said that some thirty Jewish refugees who had crossed into Slovakia from Poland had been stopped by the police

about a hundred kilometers from Bratislava and were to
be sent back to Poland. He asked if I could do anything
to help them.

The American UNRRA chief was sympathetic. He suggested that I try to see the Minister of the Slovak Ministry
of the Interior since that department controls the police.
He offered me a car and the services of his Czech secretary.

In Slovakia, which has considerable autonomy within
the Czechoslovak state, the government is about two-thirds
Democratic and one-third Communist. The Democrats
number some democratic elements but are chiefly reactionary, undemocratic, and anti-Semitic. Some of their
election leaflets looked as if they might have been prepared by the Nazis.

Fortunately for the refugees, the Ministry of the Interior is in the hands of the communists. Dr. Julius Viktory, the Minister, agreed to see me. Through my Czech
interpreter I told him that I was an American newspaper
correspondent telling the story of the illegal Jewish emigration. I said I was impressed with the kindness the
Czechs were showing to the Jews. I informed him that I
had heard that morning of the case of thirty Jews who
were being refused passage by the Slovak police and
ordered back to Poland. I declared that I would regret
having to make an unfavorable report on the treatment
of Jewish refugees in Slovakia and asked what was going
to be done with the detained group.

Dr. Viktory assured me that as an anti-Fascist he understood the problem facing the Jews of Eastern Europe, that
he was sympathetic.

"I am sending orders to the local police," he went on, "instructing them to release the refugees and to allow them to proceed to Bratislava on their way across Slovakia to Vienna."

I thanked Dr. Viktory. I just had time to join the illegal transport for Vienna.

III

At the hotel I changed into civilian clothes, but left off my necktie to look less respectable. At the Hotel Jelen. I learned that the refugees had already started for the railroad station, but I caught up with them.

At the station I found that the original fifty with whom I had traveled from Anton had been increased by two hundred more refugees who had come into Bratislava by various means and from many points on the Polish-Czechoslovak border. Four old freight cars were waiting for us. They were attached to the end of a local train and had been arranged for by UNRRA. We all climbed up in a happy mood and made ourselves as comfortable as we could. There were twenty-five children among the two hundred and fifty. The youngest, a child of three months, was being suckled by its mother when we entered our car.

The *khalutsim* were excited to see me again. They all began talking at once. A *Haganah* worker we had not seen before came up and warned us to be quiet. He told

us that we were supposed to be natives of the country of
Z————. He said we were to speak only Hebrew, not
Yiddish. The Yiddish was recognizable because of its
high German content, but the Hebrew would sound
strange enough to pass for the language of that far country, Z————.

Our new escort was a young Hungarian Jew, an ex-
partisan who had later become a *Haganah* man, a sturdy
chap, lively and full of fun. He was very popular with
the frontier guards. He made the trip from Vienna to
Bratislava every other day, taking a party of refugees
across the border each time he returned to Austria.

He told us that so many Jews had crossed that border
as natives of Z————, all of them speaking Hebrew,
that occasional groups of Z————'s found things difficult. On one occasion a number of Z————'s arrived
at the border with authentic repatriation papers. The
guards were used to seeing the somewhat less than genuine documents carried by Jewish refugees and became
suspicious. To test the Z————'s the guards asked:

"How do you say 'good evening' in the Z————
language?"

The Z————'s all said good evening in their own
tongue.

"Aha," said the guards, "we thought there was something odd about this party. The way to say good evening
in Z———— is *erev tov.*"

Erev tov is good evening in Hebrew.

The escort spoke Hungarian, Hebrew, a little English,
but he knew no Yiddish. In his khaki shirt and trousers,

with his face tanned by the sun, and his informal manner, he could easily have passed for a typical American boy. He told us that one time when he was convoying a group of Jews pretending to be Z————'s he ran into a policeman who knew a Z———— living in that town. The policeman called the Z———— over and said:

"Here are some of your compatriots."

The Z———— began to talk in his own language.

"I didn't know what to do," our escort said. "I was afraid we were in for trouble. I started talking Hebrew as fast as I could to the Z————, but I interspersed it with the name of the most northerly province of Z———— where the people speak a different dialect. I kept saying I was from that province. All he could catch was the name of the province. Finally he turned to the policeman and said: 'These are Z————'s all right, but they come from the province of X where they speak a different dialect.'

"I assure you," said the *Haganah* worker, "I was in quite a sweat by the time that conversation was over."

Three-quarters of an hour after we left Bratislava we reached the end of the line in Slovakia. We got off at a small station about four kilometers from the border. Our *sheliakh* led us quickly out of the station by a side gate before any questions could be asked, and down a dusty road in the hot afternoon sun. Near me marched a young mother, barefoot, with her baby tied to her back papoose fashion. At one point a few ducks joined the procession and waddled along in great dignity beside us.

We stopped beside a brook where there was a patch

of grass and trees. There we all put down our bags and
rested while the *sheliakh* dickered with a peasant for two
carts to carry the bags, the children and the sick. We were
all supposed to chip in to pay the cost but it took a lot of
scolding by the *Haganah* man to make some of the refugees part with a contribution from their meager funds.

Most of us stretched out for a rest on the grass while
we waited. A half dozen peasant children and two gypsies
looked on curiously. Two peasant women, their skirts
rolled up, went on calmly washing clothes in the nearby
brook.

When the *sheliakh* finally finished haggling with the
peasant, the carts were loaded and forded across the brook.
We marched across single file over a narrow wooden
plank and formed in rows of five on the other side for
our march to the border.

I must say a word about our luggage, which was the
oddest assortment of knapsacks, handbags, paper bags,
burlap bags, and old suitcases I have ever seen. The
luggage was no stranger than we were. In the front row,
as we began to march forward, was an old grandfather
with a beard. He had an extra pair of shoes hanging over
his shoulder. In the rear was a very fat woman who limped
along in ill-fitting shoes and carried an ancient black
umbrella as a parasol against the sun. Most of us had two
loaves of bread each slung over our shoulders, these being
the principal rations handed out at the Hotel Jelen for
our journey.

Ahead of us was a small village. We started down the
dusty main street in silence. Dogs began barking as we

went by. Geese honked and roosters crowed, a cow ambled
down a side street and stood watching us placidly as we
went by. An elderly peasant sat outside his house peacefully smoking a long pipe. A kind-hearted peasant woman
began to pump at a well along the street and offered us
water. Many broke ranks to have a drink.

It was very hot, but many of us wore not only coats
but all the belongings we could possibly wear, as one way
of carrying them across the border. I had on a shabby blue
raincoat to hide my too respectable looking brown tweed
suit.

Sweat poured from us. The gravel crunched beneath
our feet. I don't think I shall ever forget that steady
tramp, tramp, tramp as we marched toward the border.

We soon left the village and proceeded over a rough
stone causeway to the Czech-Austrian frontier barrier. On
the left were mountains. On the right cows grazed in a
sunken meadow. The children grinned happily from the
top of the luggage piled in the two carts at the head of
the procession, which came to a halt at the gates.

IV

On the other side of the barrier on the Czech-
Austrian border was a long bridge across what seemed
to be an extensive marsh, with a sluggish river running
through it. Three Czech officers sat on the railing. Al-

though this was the boundary of the Russian zone of
Austria, no Russians or Austrians were in sight.

This is the way we got across: Our Hungarian friend
had a list of all us Z————'s on official looking sta-
tionery. As he read each name the person whose name
was called would answer and run across the border. The
names were typically Jewish—Rosenblum, Yacob; Adler,
Rifkah; Abramovitch, Itzik—and these created a good
deal of amusement among the Czech officers lounging on
the railing, because they knew that these were hardly the
names of Z————'s.

A cool breeze blew over the frontier bridge as we
waited. The Hungarian *sheliakh* was supposed to call out
my name at some point, as though I too were on the list.
I waited until about two-thirds of the refugees had gone
over, growing more and more restless. I was afraid he
might have forgotten me. When he called out "Bromov,
Moishe," and no Moishe Bromov answered, I seized the
opportunity. I ran up to the border, said I was Moishe
Bromov, and passed over to the other side. I never found
out what happened to the real Moishe Bromov.

When we had all gotten across, we proceeded with our
march. This passage through Mr. Churchill's "iron curtain" was the easiest frontier crossing on my entire trip.
We seemed to have stirred little curiosity on the Russian
side.

Our first contact with the Russians occurred when we
made way for a Russian officer riding by on horseback.
At one point we passed a playing field where Russian
soldiers were playing English-style football. Two carriages

passed us, with Russian soldiers and their *Fräulein* friends
out for a gay afternoon. Near the railroad station on the
Austrian side, a group of Russian soldiers and officers
stood along the road to watch us go by, but no questions
were asked.

About four kilometers from the border, we arrived at a
railroad station, where our bags were unloaded and we
picked them up and crowded into third-class carriages,
headed for Vienna. It was about four o'clock in the afternoon.

For some reason, perhaps out of the misguided notion
that I preferred to travel with the better element, the
sheliakh ushered me up to the first third-class carriage
where he saw to it that the one obviously well-to-do refugee family and I had a whole compartment to ourselves.
I was annoyed because I really wanted to be with my
khalutsim.

The head of the prosperous family was a pretentious
Polish Jew who wore a good suit of clothes, pince-nez
glasses and a pompous air. He had once been to America
and imagined that he could speak English, which he
would attempt to do with the slightest encouragement.
His buxom wife assumed the expression of a lady who
wanted everyone to understand that she might swoon at
any moment. Somehow she had managed to get to the
border with a wrist watch and three diamond rings. On
her feet she wore a huge pair of high men's shoes, black
and dirty, with round stubbed toes of the kind one usually
associates with stevedores. With these two *pritsim* [Yid-
dish slang for would-be aristocrats] was their well-dressed,

pretty daughter, who was accompanied by her young husband.

Before the train started I stuck my head out of the window and waved frantically to attract the attention of the *khalutsim*. Two of them ran up to join me. I had missed lunch because of my interview with the Slovak minister. We got out the salami and a penknife. The *khalutsim* had a big loaf of bread and we started to eat. I could see that the mouths of our dignified friends were watering and offered them salami. They all accepted except the mother, who looked as if she wouldn't think of eating any such horrible stuff, especially when it was cut by a dirty penknife.

At every stop, and there were many, more *khalutsim* ran up to join me and the salami. The lady was horrified by my disreputable friends.

At 5:15 we changed trains at Ganserndorf. The station had been badly bombed. Here we lost the luxury of our third-class compartment and were packed in among a lot of annoyed Austrian peasants and working people. I sat on my bags in the vestibule. There must have been eight of us squeezed in with our bags on that little platform.

Near me stood an elderly, haggard little hunchback. He was dirty and very weary. He was about five feet tall and wore a Russian workman's cap. I didn't know whether he was an Austrian workman or a Jewish refugee and I asked one of the other passengers if he was "one of us." I was told he was. I took the remains of my salami out of my bag, cut off a thick slice and offered it to him with a piece of bread. He thanked me in Yiddish and put the food carefully away in his bag to eat later. We began talking; he told me he was a Polish Jew who had been in Russia during the war. He had worked as a postman among the collective settlements in the countryside.

Almost every refugee carries, hidden away on him like some precious possession, a grubby notebook in which he has the names and addresses of relatives and friends, and he will ask if you know so and so in "Chicago" and "Neff York." The little hunchback was no exception.

His name was Schloime Weisman and he came from Brok nach Bugiem in Poland. He wanted to know whether I knew a Rabbi Jacob M. Pomerance. The only address he had for him was Brooklyn 6, New York. I told him I didn't. He then confided that the rabbi and he had gone to the same theological seminary.

"What did you do before the war?" I asked Weisman.

"*Gelernt* [studied]" was the answer.

The one word carried a world of satisfaction. He had been in a *yeshiva* [theological seminary] when the war began.

"Hard work," he added, ironically.

"Where are you headed now?" I wanted to know.

The tired face lit up with a happy smile.

"*Eretz.*" ("Palestine").

After much coaxing I got him to take my seat on the bag. I climbed outside the train onto the roof, which was cool and comfortable provided one kept an eye out for the low bridges.

On the roof with me was a seventeen-year-old *khaluts* from Poland, a boy with glasses and a thin, intellectual face. He told me he and his parents had come from Russia and that he had left them behind to go to Palestine.

"Look," he said to me, pointing proudly. "I have this jacket, this shirt, these pants, socks, and shoes. I brought nothing more."

"Well," I said, "I've got a lot of shirts in my bag and the darned thing's too full. How about taking a couple of my shirts?"

"No," he said, with a grand gesture. "A *khaluts* needs nothing."

When I told him I had been to Palestine the year before he insisted that I tell him about the colonies.

So we entered Vienna. We got off the train at Floridsdorf near one of the groups of workers' apartments which had been shelled by Dollfuss and had never been repaired.

There, before the startled eyes of a group of Austrian workmen, we were lined up and marched off quickly to a corner where our Hungarian *sheliakh* jammed us into two trolley cars linked together. The trolleys took us from the Russian to the American zone.

V

Vienna reminded me of an American ghost town of vast dimensions. It was not as badly damaged as the German cities I had seen, but the damage here seemed spiritual as well as physical. Munich and Nuremberg could be rebuilt in a quarter-century, but one had the feeling that the harm done Vienna was irreparable, that it would never emerge from its lesser ruins.

The scarred workers' homes we first saw at Floridsdorf were more than the wreckage of a co-operative venture in public housing—they represented the end of what was once one of the most promising working-class movements in Europe. The bomb-mangled splendor of the Ring, the famous boulevard that encircles inner Vienna, already had the aspect of a museum exhibit. The Ring is the heart of a vanished empire that seems remarkably benevolent and well ordered in retrospect. The peoples over which the Hapsburgs once ruled are poisoned by mutual hatreds: Czech against Slovak, Pole against Czech, Slovak against Maygar, Croat against Serb.

To stand in the cool of an early morning in the green park of the *Rathausplatz,* the city hall plaza, and look toward the delicate spires of the *Votivkirche*—the church the Emperor Franz Josef built in gratitude for his escape from assassination — is to get a glimpse of battered Vienna's one-time imperial splendor. It is somewhat over-adorned and not quite in the best taste, but massively impressive. In front of the vast Hofburg palace, a small imitation Greek temple carries an inscription which still proclaims, in a small quaint voice: *"Justitia Regnorum Fundamentum."* [Justice is the foundation of kingdoms.] Nearby, on the Ring, covering part of the front of the national school headquarters, huge pictures of Lenin and Stalin proclaim a new order beyond the wildest night-mares of Franz Josef.

Opposite the Parliament House with its white angels and black horses, which looks a little as though it had been designed by a pastry cook, one can see the graves of nine Red Army heroes in the Volksgarten. At seven in the morning, many Viennese were already sitting amid the deep shade and singing birds. There were floral wreaths at the base of the monuments on the Russian graves, several of which carried pictures of the departed. The strange-looking Russian characters noted that they fell in the struggle against Fascism.

This Vienna, which begins to seem more a relic than a living city despite the trams and hurrying people in the streets, is the great crossroads of the Jewish exodus from Central and Eastern Europe, an exodus that is greater in magnitude, misery, and drama than those from Egypt and Spain.

The center of Jewish life in Vienna today is the huge Rothschild Memorial Hospital. Its squalor and vitality contrast with the faded loveliness of the city. When we marched up, the sidewalk and the steps were crowded with refugees waiting to greet any friends, relatives, or comrades they might find among the newcomers. There were cries of joy, kisses and hugs, when some of those waiting recognized people they knew in our group.

The hospital was bombed during the war and has yet to be completely repaired. It would be a rather gloomy, cavernous place were it not for the people who mill about in the corridors and stroll in the inner courtyard, gossiping cheerfully in Yiddish. Once arrived at the Rothschild Hospital, refugees feel themselves in friendly territory.

We were shepherded through the crowds and down a dark staircase into a basement full of people. We passed rooms used as a trades school and as repair shops for shoes and clothing into a large room for our médical examinations. After the medical examination we had to fill out an Army DP registration questionnaire. Among other things this recorded "Claimed Nationality," "Religion (optional)," "Last Permanent Residence or Residence January 1, 1938," "Desired Destination," "Usual Trade, Occupation or Profession," and "Languages Spoken in Order of Fluency." When this had been filled out each refugee received an identity card, with a name and number.

It is difficult for Americans, accustomed to move freely without passports through most of North America, to appreciate what it means to get this document. In Europe today even legal travelers must have papers of many different kinds. The need for *Papiere* clogs the wheels of commerce and makes business in Europe an exasperating affair for businessmen.

To march across borders illegally, stateless and homeless, without documents, and then to come at last to a place where one meets a friendly reception, where one is given an identity card, is something only a refugee can fully appreciate. One suddenly becomes a person, with a name, a number, and a *paper*. One now has a right to move freely in the American zone of Austria. This privilege and this blessing the Jewish refugee owes to the American occupying forces. In spite of the complaints and occasional clashes between DP's and the military police, the United States Army is the best friend the Jewish

people have in Europe today. I cannot speak too highly
of the efficiency and the kindness with which General
Mark Clark and Brigadier General Ralph H. Tate, deputy
commanding general of the United States Forces in Austria, treat refugees coming out of Eastern Europe.

In the corridors of the Rothschild Hospital were Jews
from Rumania, Hungary, Slovakia, Greece, and Yugoslavia as well as Poland. I also spoke there one evening
with a small delegation representing the Jews of Vienna.
These alone seemed pathetic. Before the war there were
two hundred thousand Jews in Vienna. The Hapsburgs
were tolerant monarchs. Jews played a great part in the
life of the city. Many were converted to Catholicism. The
Jews were important in the city's cultural as well as its
business life. The delegation, all elderly and gentle folk,
told me there were twenty thousand Jews and half-Jews,
including the Catholic Jews, left in Vienna.

Of these twenty thousand, only four thousand are people
both of whose parents were Jewish and who count themselves as of the Jewish faith. More than half of the four
thousand are over forty-five years of age.

"There are few young people left and these are emi-
grating," one member of the delegation told me. "We
who remain are folk too old to begin life again somewhere else. We love Vienna, but there will soon be no
Jews left in it. Anti-Semitism grew very strong under the
Nazis and during the war, and there is no future here for
the younger people."

For me, the most fascinating place in Vienna was the
Jewish soldiers' club. It seemed to be the one place in the

capital where the Jewish officers and men of the four occupying powers meet socially.

I met a big strapping fellow there in a Scotch Highlander uniform who had enlisted in the British Army at the beginning of the war and been assigned to a Scotch regiment. He was a *sabra*. *Sabra* means cactus in Hebrew; it is the slang term applied to denote native-born Palestinians; they are supposed to be like the cactus, prickly without but sweet within.

I heard an American lieutenant having a typical GI argument in Brooklyn Yiddish with a Red Army officer who spoke Litvak Yiddish. The American wanted to know why the Russian soldiers weren't cleaner and better dressed. The Russian retorted angrily that his comrades had been fighting a war on inadequate resources and under conditions that did not allow them to dress up.

"Our men," he concluded nastily, "didn't come here to fraternize with *Fräuleins*."

The Russian Jewish soldiers were intensely interested in Palestine. One Red Army major asked many questions about my trip to Palestine the year before.

"I'm a communist. I'm not a Zionist. But we must support the building of Palestine. For many Jews in Eastern Europe west of the Soviet border there is no other way out," he said.

Another repeated to me with pride the famous remark made by the Soviet Union's former Ambassador to Britain, Maisky, who commented after a visit to the Jewish collective settlements in the Holy Land, "We have reached socialism, but you have already achieved communism."

VI

The Rothschild Memorial Hospital was run by a combination of three agencies, the DP division of USFA,
UNRRA, and a Jewish committee representing the DP's
themselves, with aid from the American Jewish Joint
Distribution Committee.

This committee was headed by a Polish Jew named
Teicholz, a vigorous, cheerful man in his middle thirties
of considerable executive capacity. I first met him on the
Orient Express from Paris on my way to Stuttgart, two
weeks before I got to Czechoslovakia. He was a leader of
the Jewish resistance movement in Hungary and was part
of the network which helped Jews to escape from Hitler-
occupied Europe.

He told me one of the rare stories I heard of Germans
helping Jews during the war. He was once captured by
SS men on the Hungarian border. He had false Aryan
papers but the SS suspected he was a Jew. A Wehrmacht
doctor came along and said he would examine Teicholz
to see whether or not he was circumcized. (Circumcision
among Gentiles is far less common in Europe than in
America.)

"The doctor took me into a hut on the border," Teicholz
related. "He saw that I was circumcized, but he picked
up the phone to the frontier station nearby and said, 'This
man is an Aryan'."

"Did the doctor say anything to you?" I asked.

"All he did was shake my hand as I went out," Teicholz told me. "He was an elderly man with a sensitive face. He saved my life. The SS men sent me with the Aryan prisoners to a work camp from which I later escaped. Otherwise I would have gone with other Jews to the gas chamber. Jews caught on the border didn't have a chance."

At a concert and entertainment given by the DP's at Rothschild Hospital I met a man who had worked with Teicholz in the underground. He was a Red Army officer with three medals: the Stalin medal, and the Budapest and Vienna medals. He was a slim young man with tanned features and blue eyes and he told me that he had recently been demoted to *Unteroffizier*. He had been in charge of a concentration camp in Czechoslovakia for captured SS men. There were twenty-five hundred SS men in his camp, and he and the sixty soldiers under him had killed every one of the twenty-five hundred in two weeks. His punishment was the demotion, but he did not look as though he regretted it.

He was a Russian Jew who had been dropped by parachute on Hungarian territory in 1942 to organize partisan bands. On the side he helped the Jewish underground. The Red Army trained him carefully for this mission. He spoke both Hungarian and German and had false papers and false uniforms. He operated as an SS man and as an Hungarian army officer. The stories he told sounded incredible, but Teicholz assured me they were true.

"On one occasion," the Red Army man said, "I walked into a concentration camp in SS uniform, picked out six

Jews, said 'I want those blankety blank Jews for a purpose they won't like at all' and took them out of the
camp. When we got away I turned them over to the Jewish underground, which succeeded in smuggling them out
of the country to allied territory."

He was a patriotic Russian and I saw tears in his eyes
at the concert when one artist sang a Russian Yiddish
song:

> *Ikh benk nokh mayn Russishe heym,*
> *Nokh mayne Russishe bruder*
> *Nokh mayne hartslikhe Russishe lider.*
> [I long for my Russian home,
> For my Russian brothers,
> For my heart-warming Russian songs.]

He called himself a Zionist and said he was strongly
in favor of helping to build up Palestine as a home for
the Jews of Central and Eastern Europe.

I met a non-Jewish illegal immigrant to Palestine in
Teicholz's office at the hospital. She was a short, dumpy,
middle-aged woman, a Pole from Galicia. Her name had
been Franciska Lorzy but she had changed it to Clara
Plitzer, a Jewish name. She was the widow of a farm
laborer, a good-hearted motherly woman.

During the war she had saved two Jewish boys from the
Nazis. Both were sons of Jewish friends. When these
friends were sent into the ghetto by the Nazis in 1941
the boys were left in her keeping. One was five, the other
four. The Germans killed both parents. After the war the
older boy was taken by the Jewish community to be

trained as a *khaluts.* The younger one, now eight years old, was with her; she had refused to give him up.

"I told them I didn't mind his becoming a *khaluts* and going to Palestine," she said, "but he's all I have left in the world and I'm going with him."

She took the boy's last name as her own and adopted the name Clara because she thought it sounded more Jewish than Franciska. She had been granted an illegal immigration certificate by the underground.

VII

I checked in at the Weisse Hahn, the press camp of the U. S. Forces in Austria, and got into touch with a *Haganah* representative. I was told to be ready to leave in twenty-four hours. Word had come that I was to fly back to France, where another underground agent would take me to a seacoast from which an illegal ship was scheduled to sail within a short time.

The *khalutsim* with whom I had traveled from Bratislava had been transferred from the Rothschild Memorial Hospital to a hostel on the Alserbachstrasse. I went there to say good-by to them before leaving. A radio was blaring away in the inner courtyard when I got there and refugees were busily at work repaving the court with bricks. The hostel held about 5,000 refugees and in an upstairs barracks I received a joyful welcome from my young comrades.

They introduced me to ten other comrades from their group at the *Kibbutz Dror* in Poland who had arrived a few days ahead of them. They did not know at that time whether they were to be distributed with other refugees to camps in the American zones of Austria and Germany, or whether as *khalutsim* they were to be smuggled over the border into a neighboring country for transportation to Palestine. To go to the camps meant a long wait, while the interminable negotiations went on between Britain and America for their admission to Palestine. To go over the border by certain mountain passes known to the underground was to have a chance to reach Palestine within a few weeks or months by illegal ship.

I warned my young friends that they might have a long wait and urged them to keep their spirits up if they found themselves in a German or Austrian DP camp. I asked them to write me, and our leave-taking was rather tearful all around. I later heard that they were among the fortunate who went ahead and that they reached Palestine safely.

My plane out of Vienna was grounded by engine trouble in Salzburg, in as lovely an airfield as I have ever seen, a bowl among the Austrian Alps. There I telephoned Leon D. Fisher, a young New Yorker who works for the Joint Distribution Committee in Salzburg. He is a professional social worker and psychiatrist.

He picked me up at the airport in a jeep and told me about the work and the camps in the American zone. The model camp of the area, and probably the one place in the world where Jewish or any other refugees really have luxurious surroundings, was at Bad Gastein, a famous watering place where the Army took over five large hotels to house DP's.

There were fourteen hundred refugees at Bad Gastein. Camp New Palestine in Salzburg, which housed four hundred and fifty people, was the next best known hostel. The largest camp was Bindermichel, which has twenty-four hundred people. About two hundred refugees are billeted in private homes in Salzburg. There are accommodations for two hundred at the transient camp in Enns.

One hundred and fifty tubercular DP's were being cared for at a hospital in the American zone.

The Jewish population in the American zone in Austria had increased from fifteen thousand to over thirty-four thousand. Three thousand were in the British zone and one thousand in the French. Conditions were good in the latter, although food was scarce.

A DP in Salzburg said that he was one of a group of eighty Jews from Poland, Hungary, and Rumania who had made their way across Austria. They had no difficulties in the Russian zone, but at Furstenfeld, in the English zone, they were stopped and four of their number arrested. The rest refused to go on until the four were released. Late in the afternoon they demonstrated outside the British headquarters; soldiers with bayonets fired guns over their heads to stop them, and arrested four more.

"In the British prison," one man related, "I found an SS *Obersturmführer* and nine Jews who had been taken from a previous illegal transport of a hundred and seventy. We were questioned about the illegal immigration.

"The British wanted to know how we got across the border, who led us across, how we made contact with the underground, and many other things. We told them nothing. Finally they released us."

Fisher told me that the work of the Joint Distribution Committee in caring for refugees around Salzburg was greatly helped by the friendly attitude of the Forty-Second Division under General Harry Collins. He especially praised the DP section of the Forty-Second, which was under Major A. D. Schutz.

New Palestine, in the shadow of the Alps on the outskirts of Salzburg, looked like a model village housing development. During the occupation it was an SS troop residence. Now the Jewish flag, the blue and white *Mogen Dovid* of Palestine and the Zionist movement, flies over the settlement.

Fisher was particularly proud of a Jewish children's home at St. Gilgen, high up in the Austrian Alps. We drove out to see it, past Ribbentrop's summer home. The countryside was unbelievably beautiful.

We passed a chain of aquamarine lakes set like jewels amid the green, grizzly bear mountains. There is an officers' rest camp at nearby Frischl.

The children's home was a wealthy Nazi's villa. It is high up on a mountainside and overlooks one of the lakes. Fifty children from various DP camps in Austria spend two weeks each at the home. One of the youngsters confided that he wanted to be a newspaperman. I gave him my Palestinian press card, which bore the date of my first

visit to Palestine in 1945 and was printed in English,
Arabic and Hebrew.

"Now," I said, "you can go to Palestine legally as a
newspaperman."

The other children crowded around to see this memento
of the Holy Land.

The next morning a Red Cross executive with whom
I was traveling borrowed a jeep and we crossed the Austrian border to Berchtesgaden to see Hitler's hideaway.

The countryside through which we drove was Wag-
nerian in its lofty, turgid beauty.

The Hitler house was a wreck. Allied bombers and sou-
venvir hunters had left little behind them. The walls were
covered with the handwriting of GI's and the *Mogen
Dovids* of American Jewish soldiers. On the second floor,
in the huge victory hall, the whole side of one wall had
held one great window overlooking the Alps. The view
made megalomania almost inescapable for anyone who
lived there. Solemnly I committed a primitive act of contempt.

On the way back we passed an SS prisoners' camp with
a double row of barbed wire, watchtowers, and searchlights. SS men were stretched out enjoying a sunbath.

"As far as they're concerned," said the Red Cross man,
"it's an ideal place in which to relax and plan for the
future."

Adventure in Italy

I

I flew to X——— from Salzburg and out again in twenty-four hours. I was told that an illegal ship, the *Haganah,* was to leave a south European port within a matter of hours.

I was given a hilarious welcome when I arrived. The crew members I had seen on that memorable night back home thumped me on the back and shouted "Izzy, we knew you'd make it." They assigned me a bunk in the officers' cabin, and one of the boys loaned me an old pair of dungarees to wear on deck.

But the *Aliyah Beth* timetable had again gone awry.

There were mysterious delays. There were whispers among the crew that difficulties had cropped up on a high level. The ex-Mufti had just escaped from Paris and there was speculation that our delay was somehow connected with that escape.

I spent some time visiting the training centers for illegal immigrants in the neighborhood. In these were classes in farming, various manual trades and Hebrew—for Hebrew is the principal language of the Jews in Palestine.

One *hachshara* [training camp] was nothing more than a miserable collection of barracks behind barbed wire which had been used as a detention camp for German prisoners of war. Others were makeshift quarters in little fishing settlements along the sea. The prize of the lot was in an ex-collaborator's villa, high up on a mountain overlooking the seacoast. Here I talked and swam with *khalutsim* from almost every country in Europe, and I was later to travel with many of them to Palestine.

These visits were pleasant, but as day followed day with no prospect of sailing, I grew impatient. I began to be afraid that my newspaper would call me home before I completed the journey. One Sunday morning a worker of the *Haganah* arrived with the news that a refugee ship would leave a small port in Italy the following Tuesday night.

Fortunately I had a visa. I was told how I could contact the underground in that port.

When I arrived at N——— I checked in at a hotel and made for the waterfront. The ship was the *Sir Josiah Wedgewood*, a sister ship of the one I had just left. It was

named for a famous champion of Zionism in the British
Labor Party, a man who suggested to Jewish leaders long
before the war that they ignore British immigration re-
strictions and take *khalutsim* illegally to Palestine.

The *Haganah* and the *Sir Josiah Wedgewood* were
750-ton ships, formerly in the Canadian Navy. Both ships
have since been captured by the British, while taking immigrants to Palestine.

I did not locate the *Sir Josiah* until I found an Italian
workingman who understood enough French to lead me
to the ship.

A gangplank led at a rather dizzy incline from the
wharf to the stern deck of the boat. A thin faced boy in
glasses whom I had met in the United States stood on
guard to prevent strangers from going aboard. I recognized Jay at once, but he didn't recognize me.

I was wearing a Basque beret which I had acquired
under hypnotic suggestion from a gifted salesman several
days earlier, a Turkish-born French Jew known to the
Americans as Joe. I wore the beret with civilian clothes
in Italy and there I was taken for a Frenchman.

Since the beret seemed to have confused Jay, too, I
thought I'd have some fun at his expense. Like many
practical jokes, this one almost ended badly.

I walked around the wharf, looking the boat over with
what was intended to be a knowing expression. I said, in
what I hoped would sound like French to Brooklyn-bred
ears:

"*Un étrange bateau, un étrange bateau.*"

The sentry was worried.

I asked: *"Où est le capitaine?"*

The captain, I learned later, was listening from the deck but said nothing.

"Who wants to see him?" the sentry asked in English.

I didn't answer. I started walking up the gangplank. Jay stopped me and asked angrily:

"Who are you? What's your name?"

I said my name was Jacques Pirandel and added that I was from the *Deuxième Bureau*. The *Deuxième Bureau* is the FBI of France.

The sentry looked a little green around the gills.

My *Haganah* contact had instructed me to ask for any one of three people when I found the ship in N————. One was the captain, whom I had met in America. The other two were Giacomo and Pietro.

Pietro is the name of a *Haganah* worker. Giacomo is a former Partisan leader who has been very helpful to Jewish refugees. When I asked for Giacomo the sentry took me to his house near the waterfront.

My beret and bad French worried Giacomo, too, and he marched me back to the boat. Near the boat were waterfront saloons in which some of Giacomo's former Partisan followers passed much of their time in order to keep a protective eye on any illegal Jewish boats that happened to be in the harbor.

I was beginning to be worried. I had expected to be recognized sooner. I didn't want to start by giving everybody a bad fright and getting in wrong with the crew and their underground friends. I didn't know until afterwards that I might also have been in for some rough third degree from Giacomo's waterfront gang. On the way back we met another crew member who wanted to know just why I was interested in that boat.

"I'll show you what my interest is," I said, and burst out laughing. I pulled out a *PM* reporter's card with my name on it. The crew member was a *PM* reader and he laughed too. The matter was explained to Giacomo and I was allowed on board. Of course the crew members insisted:

"We knew it was you all the time."

I got to know Giacomo well. He had once been a seaman, and like many seamen he was very well read. He had quite a library, which he showed me proudly. Conrad and Jack London were two of his favorites and I gave him a copy of *Moby-Dick* before I left.

I was to have an exciting adventure in this ancient seafaring town.

I had two companions. One was a gentle, slender, darkhaired woman who was the widow of a gifted Italian Jew who had emigrated to Palestine in the early twenties and become one of the most inspiring leaders the Zionist movement has known. I met American boys later, on one of the illegal ships, who told me that they had once heard him speak and that it was for them an unforgettable experience.

He was captured and executed by the Nazis during the war when he was parachuted behind the German lines in Italy. After the war his widow went to Italy to try to find some trace of relatives. I had written her in Rome asking her to join me as Italian translator.

My other companion was a man known locally as Phil. He was of medium height with a strong face, graying hair and a resourceful manner. Phil came up to me in the lobby of the hotel shortly after I arrived and before I quite knew what I was doing I had hired him. as a second translator and general handyman. He spoke virtually all the East and Central European languages I was to encounter among the refugees, and assured me that he could make himself generally useful. This was no idle sales talk, as events were to show.

I had been told to keep away from the ship the day after my arrival, but to come with my companions to Giacomo's house at seven the next night.

With Giacomo were two of his Partisan followers and the chief *sheliakh* called Pietro. We went down to the harbor and waited for the boat to sail.

The Partisans seemed to be upset about some last-minute difficulties, but at 8 P.M. the ship began to move out of the harbor.

I was to sail on that boat. But it had been feared that if I boarded the ship in the town it might arouse suspicion since no passengers were mentioned in her clearance papers. The plan, then, called for my going aboard later that night at a point farther down the Italian shore, about fifty kilometers from the town. There the ship was to pick up twelve hundred *khalutsim* and I was to embark with them.

In the meantime Mrs. A———, Phil, and I went sightseeing while Giacomo and the *sheliakh* started off to the appointed rendezvous by a route of their own. Our pur-

pose in sightseeing was to throw the police off our trail
in case we were being shadowed. I took Mrs. A———— and
Phil to see a medieval alley I had discovered earlier in the
day. The alley, its high, almost windowless dwellings still
inhabited, bore the name *Vico della Crema, gia Vico dei
Giudei* [Cream Alley, formerly the Alley of the Jews].
It had been the ghetto of the city in the Middle Ages.

We drove from the ghetto to a nearby town, in a car
I had hired. There we had a leisurely dinner in an open
garden and came back along a narrow winding road where
we could easily see if anyone was following us. Apparently
no one was.

We parked about a block from my hotel. I walked to
the hotel, got my bags, paid my bill and hurried back to
the car. We speeded through the town, out the ancient
Aurelian way, the Roman road still in use along the narrow and precipitous coast.

About fifty kilometers from the town we came to a
lonely strip of beach. We parked in the sand and got out
in the darkness. At this point there was an inlet deep
enough to admit a large boat. There the ship was to pick
up its passengers, and there we found Giacomo and the
Haganah worker.

II

It was shortly after midnight. Behind us, rising cliff-like
from the narrow road along the beach, were the moun-

tains of the Riviera, huge dark shapes against the sky. There were no lights along the road. All we had to see by was the faint glow of a cloudless, starry sky. We sat down to wait.

Shortly before one o'clock in the morning, far out to sea, we saw a tiny triangle of light moving toward us. The triangle was made up of three lights, one red, one green, one white; the fore, aft, and port lights of a ship moving in toward shore.

Slowly the triangle grew larger, but the ship remained invisible. It looked as if a ghost ship were moving slowly toward the beach.

About fifteen minutes later we saw a long line of twelve double headlights winding its way along the coast to the south of us.

"That," the *sheliakh* said, "must be the first convoy."

Pietro said that two convoys of twelve trucks each were to bring twelve hundred *khalutsim* for the embarkation.

The first convoy had been scheduled to arrive at 1:00 in the morning, the second at 1:30. The ship was to come in and put down its gangplank at 1:00.

The five of us stood on the beach waiting. The *sheliakh* was signaling in Morse code to the boat with a flashlight. But for some reason the boat did not come into the inlet as planned.

The truck drove off in the darkness behind us. The *khalutsim* quickly and quietly jumped off and ran down to wait on the shore. The twelve trucks drove rapidly away.

There was no noise but the crunch of gravel under hurrying feet. None of the *khalutsim* spoke. When I

walked over and whispered *sholom,* my only greeting was
an angry glare.

An hour passed with no sign of the other trucks. The
boat remained about two hundred yards off shore.

I still don't know what caused the ship's delay, but
knowing its officers I was not too surprised. For that ship
was manned by about as odd a collection of seamen as
ever sailed the seas. The oddest was an old man with a
beard, a Jewish hobo who had become a member of
Jehovah's Witnesses. The captain and the first mate were
professional sailors, and both were ex-Wobblies. They
were buddies of many sea voyages and they had the un-
mistakable flavor of the old IWW—militant and indi-
dualistic.

The first mate was one of the seamen who pulled the
swastika off the Bremen in New York harbor in 1935.

Like many of the sailors I was to meet on these illegal
ships, neither of these officers was Jewish by anything but
the accident of birth. They had little Jewish upbringing
and no Jewish education, and were, of course, not at all
religious. But they had left families in America and taken
the risk of long sentences in British prisons if caught.
They said they were "sore as a —— boil" about the treatment the Jews had received in Europe. They spoke a thick
Brooklynese, heavily seasoned with favorite GI expletives.
But their boat was shipshape and their rather conglom-
erate crew was well disciplined and obviously scared to
death of them.

"We'll make sailors of these —— landlubbers yet,"
the captain proudly told me. But I suspected that it would

not be easy to tell the captain what to do, and so I was not too surprised when the ship failed to come into the inlet at the scheduled time.

The *sheliakh* could swear very competently in half a dozen languages, too. He was furious. Giacomo was getting more and more angry and nervous. He was nervous because of the appearance along that stretch of coast of several small Italian fishing boats. These boats used searchlights for night fishing. The fish are attracted by the lights and come to the surface where they can easily be caught.

Sooner or later the fishermen could not help but become aware that something strange was going on that night on the beach. Even in the dim starlight one could see the dark forms of the *khalutsim* huddled together like a herd of seals on the shore. Anyone could see that a flashlight was signaling in code and being answered from a big boat off shore.

Finally, about three in the morning, the boat moved in, and after some angry shouting between the *sheliakh* and the captain it drifted slowly into the inlet and dropped its gangplank. The gangplank consisted of two long, heavy boards, one higher than the other. The *khalutsim* were to walk in the dark up that dizzy, uneven incline to the deck.

But at the very moment the gangplank was dropped six *carabinieri* [Italian police] sprang toward us in the darkness, shouting, *"Ragazzi, Ebrei!"* or "Hey, fellas, here are a bunch of Jews!"

III

The six Italian gendarmes descended on us just as the first *khalutsim* were about to board the boat.

We were scared. We thought the boat was lost, that all the hard work of getting it over from America and finally clearing it out of port had gone for nothing. We feared another *Fede* affair.

The illegal boat *Fede* had been caught under similar circumstances in the harbor of La Spezia. It had taken several weeks of agitation and a hunger strike by Jewish leaders in Palestine before the British military authorities in Italy had finally permitted the boat's release.

But most of all I was afraid that the *khalutsim* would make a desperate rush for the boat and that the police might begin shooting.

With Mrs. A——— as interpreter I went over to the leader of the *carabinieri,* pulled out my most impressive reporter's card, a red State Department card with a gold American eagle on it, and said:

"I want your name and rank."

This unexpected request took him by surprise. He asked why I wanted his name. I had a flashlight with me which I turned on the card.

Through Mrs. A———, I said:

"I'm an American newspaper correspondent here to cover the sailing of this ship and I want your name and rank because I'm going to cable to America a full description of what you and your men do on this beach tonight."

I began to hand out Camels, and the *carabinieri* were visibly softened. In the meantime, the girls among the *khalutsim* were beginning to board the boat. I worried about them; the gangplank was so unsteady some of them might have fallen into the water.

The officer declined to give his name. I tried a new line.

"Why not let these people go?" I asked. "They'll get away eventually, as the people on the *Fede* did. You'll just have a lot of trouble for a couple of weeks and give Italy a black eye in the American press. Let the British worry about it. Why should you?"

"I can't make a decision on so important a matter," the officer of *carabinieri* replied. "I'll have to take you down to the prefecture."

Giacomo had withdrawn to a safe distance while this was going on. But when the police officer took me off, Mrs. A——— and Phil followed. I left my bags on the beach. The *khalutsim* were still going aboard; the *carabinieri* looked on helplessly, undecided about what to do. They were afraid the prefect might decide to release the boat and they didn't know whether to stop the people from going aboard or not.

From the rear window I saw that another car had pulled away from the beach and was following us. It was Giacomo and the underground worker. They wanted to see what would happen to us and whether we would succeed in persuading the prefect to let the boat go.

IV

The sky was just beginning to show the first faint hint of dawn when we got to town. The prefecture was in what appeared to have been a *palazzo* with a big inner courtyard and an imposing broad staircase at the entrance within the court. The police station was on our right.

The officer and the sergeant on duty conversed in whispers, but we were not booked. Instead we were taken to the second floor of the building where we were ushered into a big office to wait for the prefect.

It was almost six and fully light when he arrived. He was a big, stout Italian who listened courteously while I explained that I was an American newspaper correspondent and made a plea for the release of the *Josiah Wedgewood.*

He was friendly but he seemed interested in making an impression on persons more important to his future than a stray American journalist. He picked up the phone and began to speak rapidly in Italian.

Phil leaned over to me and whispered angrily:

"He's a two-faced so-and-so. He's talking to British military headquarters at Genoa and boasting that he just captured an illegal Jewish ship about to leave for Palestine."

"Tell him," I said to the interpreter, "that I want his

name and I'm going to telephone my paper in America immediately with the story of what he's doing."

I picked up the telephone to call a friend in Paris and ask him to call the *PM* office in New York. But the prefect took the phone away from me and said I could make no calls until after the district commissioner arrived for a hearing.

I wanted to get out of that prefecture and back to the boat somehow. I was afraid it would leave without me. I told the prefect that my earphone battery was dead and that I refused to be held for a hearing since I couldn't hear well enough to defend myself.

I said I had other batteries in my bag down on the beach and insisted that I be allowed to go back there and get them. I thought that if I could reach the beach I might be able to elude the police and go aboard.

"I don't see what difference it makes," the prefect said in Italian, "since you don't understand Italian anyway and can hear your translator well enough."

"It does matter," I insisted. "It may be that the district commissioner speaks French and that I will be able to talk directly with him."

The prefect didn't know what to do. He talked to the officer of *carabinieri*.

"They're afraid you might try to escape," Mrs. A———— explained.

Phil winked at me and said to the prefect:

"Suppose you let me go down to the beach and get Mr. Stone's bags."

The prefect agreed. Phil asked for a police pass in case, as we suspected, all the roads were being watched.

"I went downstairs," Phil told me later. "The court-yard was full of *carabinieri* who tried to stop me until I showed my pass. Outside the prefecture I saw an under-ground worker. He wanted to know what had happened and said he had tried to get to the boat but had been stopped and turned back by police. I told him I had a pass and jumped in his car. I told the police who stopped us on the outskirts of town that the prefect had sent me out to the beach to get the American journalist's bags.

"At the beach I found that the second convoy of trucks had arrived about three and a half hours late. They had had engine trouble twice on the way and the whole con-voy waited for repairs. All but two *khalutsim,* who were on the beach standing guard at the gangplank, had boarded the boat. Four obviously unhappy *carabinieri* talked among themselves nearby. The *khalutsim* said everyone had got aboard safely and that the second convoy of trucks had escaped before the police could make up their minds about what to do with them.

"At this point, the *carabinieri* walked over to hear what was going on.

"I told one of the *khalutsim* to pick up your bags and carry them to the car. On the way the underground worker told him in Hebrew that he was to give the captain his orders. He was to tell the captain to drop the gangplank as soon as possible, cut the ropes, and if necessary abandon his anchor and make a run for the open sea. 'If they start shooting,' he said, 'don't pay any attention to them but keep right on going'."

From far up the road he looked back. The boat was still there, tied tightly to the shore.

V

I got tired of waiting at the police station. While the prefect was out of the office Mrs. A———and I walked out, down the stairs, and out of the courtyard full of gendarmes. They looked surprised but didn't try to stop us.

We put in a telephone call at a hotel about five blocks away. While Mrs. A——— waited I went to a sidewalk café which was just opening and ordered coffee.

A plainclothesman and two gendarmes came over, looking very ill at ease. I invited them to join me for coffee, which they did with pleasure. When Mrs. A———arrived they explained that they wanted me to go back to the prefecture with them. I said I wanted to go back anyway, but not until I had had a second cup of coffee. When I finished, we all walked out together.

Phil had already returned to the prefecture. He told me that when he arrived he found the place in great excitement. The prefect told him I had escaped, and Phil heard him giving orders on the telephone to have all roads watched for me and to have me arrested on sight and brought back.

"You'd better be careful," Phil warned the police. "You've heard of Truman, haven't you?"

The prefect said that of course he had heard of the great American president.

"Well, Stone's a famous Washington correspondent. He is a good friend of Truman's and you'd better be careful that nothing happens to him. You may find yourself in a lot of trouble with the American government."

"There followed," Phil continued, "an excited series of rapid-fire telephone conversations in Italian in which Truman [pronounced Tru-mon, with the accent on the last syllable] was repeated many times. The police were instructed to handle you carefully and to try to bring you back without placing you under arrest."

We were less concerned about my brush with the law than with the fate of the ship and its human cargo.

The gendarmes in the courtyard made way for us when we got back. The district commissioner, a short thin Italian with pince-nez that gave him an intellectual air, was waiting for us.

Phil had my bags in the prefect's office. I took a fresh earphone battery out of one of them, first rummaging around the bag and taking out my war correspondent's jacket. This I hung carelessly over the bag, with the gold United States insignia topside so the Italians could see it.

The commissioner looked at my American passport, in which I had an Italian visa. I handed him my army travel orders as a military correspondent and insisted that I wanted to put a call through to the American Embassy in Rome. He told the prefect to place the call. We had quite a chat with the commissioner about the Jewish problem in Europe and about Palestine.

"Take the case of Tel Aviv," said the commissioner, anxious to impress us with his knowledge. "A few years ago it was only a small town. Now it's a great city."

"Why," I said to Mrs. A——— admiringly, "the commissioner knows a lot about Palestine."

The commissioner was pleased.

The officer of the *carabinieri* ran into the room. The boat had gotten away, he announced.

I pretended to be furious.

"This will ruin me professionally," I shouted. "I was supposed to be on that boat. I came all the way from America to make this trip and now you've made me miss the boat. How could a boat get away from armed police on the shore? The least you can do is to get a police launch which can overtake the boat and put me on it."

"The police were helpless," the officer said. "The men on board cut the ropes and dropped the gangplank and started off before they could do anything about it. They're out beyond territorial waters now and it would be impossible to catch them."

Just then the phone rang. My call had come through. But instead of calling the American Embassy in Rome the prefect had telephoned the British military at Genoa.

I told the British major on the phone that I didn't want to talk with him, that I wanted the American Embassy, not the British military.

"You're no American," he replied. "You're a South African. I can tell by your accent."

"Then you're a helluva judge of accents," I said.

"Let me talk to the prefect," he said.

The prefect informed me the British officer had said I was a South African and a British subject, and that I was to be held for questioning by British military authorities who were already on their way from Genoa in connection with the sailing of the illegal boat.

When I heard this I insisted on going into the next room and putting on my military correspondent's uniform. I had two reasons for this. One was to help prove to the Italians that I was an American and not a British subject. The other was to hide my notes. I didn't want them to fall into British hands.

First of all I changed into army socks. I placed my notes inside these socks.

I had hardly finished changing my socks when the colonel, the officer of *carabinieri,* the prefect and a gendarme came in to watch me dress—I suppose to make sure that I wasn't hiding anything. The colonel was very much impressed with my new green officer's uniform.

In the commissioner's office I insisted that I was an American citizen and would not wait for the British military. They called the British at Genoa again. The commissioner argued something in Italian.

All I could catch was *Tutti documenti,* meaning that I had all the necessary documents to prove my identity.

"Here, they want to talk to you," the commissioner said, handing me the telephone.

A British major who explained that he used to be a

newspaperman himself asked me if I'd wait to be questioned about the sailing.

I was pretty angry by that time. I told the British officer in not very polite language that if he used to be a newspaperman himself he ought to know this was a confidential assignment and that I wouldn't tell the British a thing.

"I'm working for my paper, not British Intelligence," I shouted. "These blankety blank police have made me miss the boat. If you want to take the responsibility of ordering my arrest, go ahead and try it. I'm walking out."

I slammed the receiver.

"I don't object to being questioned by Italian police in Italy," I said to the Italians, "but I'll be damned if I'll wait to be questioned by the British. They seem to think they're running this country."

This remark went over big with the Italians.

The commissioner said I could go if I would sign a statement saying that I knew the boat was leaving.

I wrote that I not only knew the boat was leaving but that I had been sent from America to sail on it and had missed the boat because I was illegally detained by the Italian police.

The phrase "illegally detained" seemed to worry them. They argued that I had not been arrested but had twice come voluntarily to the prefecture.

I scratched out the word "illegally" and added a postscript saying that I had been very courteously treated by the Italian authorities. They were all smiles when that was translated.

They made no effort to stop us when I said, "Let's get the hell out of here."

Outside I said good-by to Mrs. A———— and Phil, jumped into a waiting car and started around the town, asking everybody we saw which was the best route to Y————. This was to give the British a false lead in the event of pursuit. I drove about ten miles out of town on the way to Y————, then took a side road in the opposite direction and late that night reached the safety of a *Haganah* headquarters.

VI

I was discouraged. There I was in an underground hideaway. It looked as though I never would succeed in making the underground trip to Palestine.

The chief underground *Haganah* emissary from Palestine in that area took a liking to me and wanted me to stay on a while with him. He was an adventurous intellectual whose escapades, when they can be told, will rival anything in Dumas. He had been assigned to underground work at the beginning of the Hitler period and had spent most of his time since then in Europe, under several dozen aliases.

I will call him Jake. He had arrived in Europe while the war was still on, and he had played his part in Allied military operations as well as in Jewish rescue work. Jake had made some amazing friends in high as well as low places.

His daring and resourcefulness, his untiring energy and the atmosphere of darkly romantic conspiracy which hung about him, appealed to his Partisan comrades. They were devoted to him. One of them said to me, "Jake's a Jewish Garibaldi."

Like many romantics, Jake regarded himself as an utter realist. He was, in fact, an extraordinarily effective person. He seemed to need little sleep and at two in the morning, when the pressure of his busy day had eased, he would drag his exhausted collaborators (and your very sleepy correspondent) to some dive for coffee, brandy, and talk. And how he could talk! He had been everywhere and read everything.

Jake had all the qualities of leadership. He could make people work outrageous hours and love it. People were proud to work with him. A love of adventure and a deep concern about human suffering were the motive springs of his character.

I was afraid that if I didn't get away soon Jake would make me forget my deadlines and go to work for him. He did his best to discourage me about the possibility of making a quick trip to Palestine. The sister ship of the boat I had helped to save was waiting in another port, but he assured me it might be weeks before it left.

"That other ship," Jake said, "is bogged down by unexpected difficulties at a very high level, as you fellows say in Washington. You might as well stay here for a while. I'm going out on a job that will make fascinating copy some day. Why don't you come along?"

The job Jake had in mind was risky, fantastic and as melodramatic as a dime novel, but if successful would be of tremendous value in further European rescue work. I suspect he succeeded. Jake's not the kind of man who permits himself to fail.

"It sounds like a wonderful story, Jake," I said, "but I'm heading back. You may be right about that other ship, but if it doesn't leave in a week I've got to fly back to America and confess that I've failed. I hate like the devil to think of walking into my office after all these weeks and telling my managing editor that I didn't get to Palestine. Maybe I'll have a lucky break yet. The whole thing might clear up. I've got to be there if that boat sails."

Jake supplied me with a car. I left at six o'clock the next morning and caught a train at the border.

I Cross
the Mediterranean

I

I reached the port in which the other ship was waiting at 10:30 that night. I checked in at a hotel and immediately went out to the boat.

I was relieved to see that it was still there, but the decks were dark and deserted. The only sound was the soft lapping of the waves against its side. I went up the gangplank to the dimly lit deck. Half the crew was celebrating in the mess.

"Izzy," they shouted, pounding me on the back, "you lucky blankety blank blank son of a blank, you're back just in time. We're sailing in the morning. Word just came that everything's cleared up. How about helping to

round up some of the fellows who are out making a night
of it? Tell them to be sure and get back to the boat early."

I made the round of the local dives with the news. The
bartenders must have thought it was some kind of V-Day.
The boys had been waiting two months for this occasion.

I went back to my hotel at two in the morning, after
far too many rounds of drinks. But I couldn't sleep. I
fretted lest some last-minute mishap might force this ship,
too, to leave without me. I finally dressed, packed my bags,
woke the sleeping night clerk, paid my bill, and returned
to the ship. A noisy party was still in progress, but I went
to sleep in my old bunk in the officers' cabin.

I awoke early and went on deck. The sky was gray and
cloudy and there was a steady drizzle. An oil barge came
alongside at nine, and while we were still taking oil a
lighter began to fill our water tanks. Everybody was tense
and worried about the possibility that our sailing might
again be postponed.

The captain was in one of his rare bad tempers. The
first engineer had not shown up; two crew members were
sent out to look for him.

We were to clear the harbor and pick up our passengers
a half day's sail away. The two crew members sent out as
a searching party were instructed to meet us there the next
morning, with or without the missing engineer.

A bakery truck drove up with a load of fresh loaves
of bread. Shortly before noon a second truck arrived with
a company of German prisoners of war who unloaded
eight crates of lifebelts and carried them up to the deck.
I never did find out how German prisoners of war came

to be loading lifebelts on an illegal boat for Jewish refugees. I thought it more discreet not to ask.

At five minutes of one the steam whistle blew and an agile crew member who used to be a Ranger in the U. S. Army climbed out on the ropes in the rain and cut away the round metal rat guards.

The compass adjusters came on board and were followed by the port pilot and his assistant. They saw crew members unpacking the lifebelts and throwing the crates on shore. The pilot smiled but made no comment. Obviously there was something odd about a big naval vessel with two dozen men in its crew which took on eight crates of lifebelts, enough for a small passenger liner.

The compass adjusters went ashore after half an hour. The pilot went up on the bridge. Crew members undid the ropes holding us to the wharf and threw them on board. We lifted our anchor. The boat began to roll gently. A tug boat came alongside. As we moved out of the harbor, the skies grew darker and a stormy north wind began to blow. We dropped the pilot and headed into rough seas.

We had a tough time of it that afternoon. The ship pitched and rolled. High dark green waves broke across our decks. I hung on to the rail on the forward deck having a wonderful time at first. I tried not to look at shipmates throwing up their lunch nearby. Soon I too began to have a strange feeling and managed to make my way to the officers' cabin and into my bunk, where I shut my eyes and tried to sleep.

I was sick, as were half the crew. I didn't get out of that

bunk until nightfall. It was my first and only bout of sea-sickness on the trip.

When I came up on deck again I found we were anchored about a mile offshore. The north wind was still blowing and a heavy rain was falling. I had on a raincoat I had taken from the slop chest and one of those big sailor rainhats that tie under the chin, the kind you see in the illustrations on Scott's emulsion.

The air was good.

We could see nothing ashore but the dark shape of a high mountain. At its foot were the few twinkling lights of a small village. There, if nothing went wrong, we were to pick up our passengers in the morning.

II

The boat was manned almost entirely by American Jews. Most of them were American born, and at least one —a young fellow from Arizona—was a third generation American. But several of them had been born in those regions of Eastern Europe from which many of our passengers were fleeing, and one of them was a fugitive from Hitlerism.

Many of the crew members were New Yorkers. Others came from Chicago, Los Angeles, Baltimore, Washington, Boston, Jersey City, and New Haven. There was a

Canadian boy from Toronto. Only our chief engineer was non-Jewish.

Most of the crew had served in the Army, Navy, or Merchant Marine during the war. Some joined the crew because they were Zionists. A lot of them were American *khalutsim* who intended to remain in the collective settlements in Palestine.

The rest were simply American sailors who happened to be Jews, boys with little if any past contact with Jewish life. They spoke neither Yiddish nor Hebrew. They were not very articulate, but for them the trip was more than a heroic adventure. They all felt deeply about the treatment of the Jews in Europe and this was their way of doing something about it.

The captain was an East European in his thirties who had spent his life in the English, American, and Scandinavian merchant marines. He had been born in a small inland town and just what attracted him to the sea is a mystery even he could not explain. He began as a messboy. He served as first mate on two American boats which carried war supplies for the Soviet Union to Murmansk. He had been torpedoed. The ship on which he was first mate was sunk in the Baltic by a German submarine. The lifeboat in which he was picked up was also sunk.

The first mate was a Bronx boy who had run away from home when he was sixteen to go to sea. He was in the Merchant Marine during the war. He was on a liberty ship on the Russian route in 1943 which split on the way back, but managed to get into English waters after three days of drifting with a flooded engine room. Again, on the

India route, he was on a torpedoed boat and spent a week in a lifeboat before he was picked up.

The second mate, whom I shall call Tom, was the son of an Austrian-born grocer in a mid-western state. He, too, had been in the Merchant Marine during the war and had risen from able-bodied seaman to third officer. He had also been in the Normany invasion. When I asked him what happened to him in the Normandy invasion, he said, "Aw, nothing," and then added reflectively, "they seemed to miss me."

Tom was one of the most interesting boys in the crew. Tall, thin, in his early twenties, he spoke neither Yiddish nor Hebrew. I used to call him a Palestinian Popeye and a *Lamedvovnik*.

Lamedvov means "thirty-six." A *Lamedvovnik* is "one of the Thirty-Six." There is a Jewish legend which says God is dissatisfied with mankind because of its cruelty, sinfulness and greed. The reason he doesn't destroy the world and start all over again is because there are thirty-six saints. Nobody knows who these saints are. Their saintliness is not at all obvious. Some are Jews. Some are Gentiles. They may be white or black. They may be learned or ignorant men. They are not necessarily pious in an ordinary sense. One may meet a *Lamedvovnik* among the lowliest folk.

The *Lamedvovnik* himself is quite unconscious of being a saint. But these thirty-six, scattered about the world, are people of such genuine, unaffected, and natural goodness of heart that God finds it worth while to let an otherwise wicked world go on for their sake.

On my trip I met a number of people I like to think of as *Lamedvovnik*. One was the little British major at the DP camp in Furth outside Nuremberg. The two Czech Jews at Anton, the old peasant woman who gave us water as we marched through her village on our way across the Austrian border, Giacomo and several of the *Haganah* underground workers in Europe, all seemed *Lamedvovniks*. Tom was another.

Tom was an experienced seaman, respected and readily obeyed by our very independent crew. On the bridge he was a full-grown man. Otherwise he was still very much a big kid. He had the sailor's distrust of people who lived on land; they and their tangled affairs bewildered him. He was always glad to get back to sea after a riotous turn on shore.

The chief engineer was a Scandinavian who had been to sea for ten years. He was in France when France fell and manned a refugee ship which took fleeing Englishmen and Frenchmen from Bordeaux to Southampton. During the occupation he lived in Denmark as a mechanic.

In 1944 he took Danish-Jewish refugees back to Sweden in small fishing boats and was unable to get back. He told me he intended to send for his wife and to settle in Palestine, where he hoped to become a farm machinery expert. He was learning Hebrew, and said that life was hard in Denmark and he thought he could do better in a new country.

One of the crew members had been a B-29 pilot. Our Canadian served in the Canadian Navy during the war. One of our able-bodied seamen had been with the U. S.

Army Air Corps in the African and Italian campaigns. A fireman had served with the U. S. Navy's Twelfth Amphibious Fleet in European waters and had given up a one-third interest in a $100,000 business to go to work for the illegal immigration. The second cook had been in the Army Air Force. The radio operator served as a Navy radar technician. One oiler had been in the medical branch of the U. S. Army with the Eleventh Armored Division and was with that division when its troops were thrown as reinforcements into the Battle of the Bulge.

Our German-born refugee had come to the United States as a refugee in 1936. He enlisted in the Army, served with the armored forces of the First Infantry and later with the Rangers. He was one of the few who survived Anzio Beachhead. His shipmates were proud of him, but it was hard to get him to talk about his experiences. He spoke of his many missions behind the German lines laconically: "Aw, it was just routine work, you don't want to hear about that." But his shipmates told me that he once lured twelve Germans over the American lines by pretending to be a *Wehrmacht* officer in the darkness.

The Ranger, as we called him, did tell me about one of his experiences which he didn't consider routine.

His outfit was destroyed during the Anzio landing. After his escape from Anzio a soldier walked up to him and asked what outfit he was in. He said, "I'm a Ranger."

"This other soldier took a look at me," he went on, "and asked, 'What's your religion?' I said, 'I'm a Jew.'

"He said, 'How come a Jew got into the Rangers?'

"I was so mad I pulled out my revolver and would have

shot him, but my buddies interfered and held my arms, and my lieutenant walked up and knocked him out with a sock on the jaw."

III

The day we were to take on our human cargo for Palestine dawned raw and windy. It was drizzling when the pilot came aboard to guide us into the port at six o'clock. Our arrival didn't arouse much curiosity; we moored alongside a battered freight terminal.

While we waited for our passengers to arrive, final preparations were made to receive them. Our boat normally carried a crew of twenty-five. By building rough, unpainted wooden bunks four and five deep in every possible bit of space below decks, and in a canvas covered false deck over the stern, we had provided cramped but adequate sleeping space for more than a thousand people. There were exactly twelve hundred and forty-seven bunks on the boat and the captain told me that if he wanted to use the forepeak locker we could accommodate as many as thirteen hundred passengers.

In a special storeroom below deck we had a huge cache of canned goods, powdered eggs and other foods, including the truckload of fresh bread we had taken on the day before. We had flour and an oven in which we expected to bake bread on the voyage with the help of experienced bakers among the refugees. In a room off the galley two huge brass kettles had been set up for the stews and thick soups which were to be the main feature of meals on board. One kettle was for the orthodox Jews who wanted only kosher food. The other kettle was for the rest of us.

Amidships on deck were special canvas covered latrines and washrooms.

A few minutes after eight one of the crew members watching on deck shouted, "Here they come." We saw a line of ten trucks heading for the freight terminal. They were open trucks jammed tight with refugees. As soon as the trucks stopped in the terminal the refugees began to jump off and to unload their baggage. They helped each other strap their bags and knapsacks on their backs and then shepherded by *shomrim* [guards] of their own they began to line up in regular ranks inside the big terminal shed.

There was a cold wind blowing, but one could never have guessed it from the expressions on the faces in the freight terminal. Crew members waved from the deck and shouted, *"Sholom."*

Every section of the ship in which there was emergency sleeping space had been given a letter of the alphabet, and every bunk a number. One member of the crew was assigned to each section and instructed to act as usher for the refugees.

On the pier each refugee was given a slip of paper with the letter of his section and the number of his bunk. This was to speed up the loading and avoid confusion. When all those waiting had been handed their slips, a signal was given to begin the embarkation.

This was the great moment for which we had all been waiting. A group of former Partisans was given the honor of being the first to come aboard the boat. I stood at the top of the gangplank on deck to lend a hand on the final steps up, because the ascent was high and shaky.

The second mate, Tom, stood down below on the deck, took the bags from the backs of the girls and threw the bags to me so the girls wouldn't have to walk up the plank burdened. The embarkation was very orderly. Groups came on board about twenty at a time so they could be taken to their bunks before a new group boarded. The first refugee to step on deck was a husky dark-haired young Partisan from Lwow named David Pickman.

There were police all over the pier and the boat. All day long we fed them in relays in the mess. They ate as if they hadn't had enough to eat in months; the local police and port officials must have consumed several weeks' provisions that morning and drunk half a case of very fine brandy which had been saved for just such an occasion. The more they ate and drank the friendlier the atmosphere became.

Below deck, the older refugees crept wearily into their bunks while the younger ones stood in the narrow aisles chatting happily among themselves in Yiddish. One group after another came on deck in a steady stream. In the freight shed hundreds waited in orderly ranks, and from time to time new trucks rumbled into the terminal.

The people coming aboard had been traveling all night

from distant camps and cities, some more than a hundred miles away. The women looked awkward, chapped and windblown after standing ten hours in an open truck, driving over rough roads in a cold, fierce, rain.

All the passengers had a tin cup and pot hanging from the rolled blanket in which they carried their belongings. There were names or initials on most of the bags and knapsacks. One woman was carrying her baggage in a burlap bag stamped "National Sugar Refining Company, New York."

The embarkation was complicated by the fact that it had to take place on a Saturday morning, and many of the passengers were orthodox Jews. One of the underground workers said there had been considerable discussion as to whether it was permissible for such a purpose to travel and to carry bags on the Sabbath, which begins at sundown Friday evening.

The majority decided that it was a *mitzva* [a pious deed] for a Jew to go to Palestine and that they would therefore be forgiven for what would ordinarily be a sin. But two members of the *Agudath Israel* stayed behind. They felt that even for such a purpose it was not proper to violate the Sabbath and that they would rather take their chances and wait for another ship.

Each group of trucks from a different camp or city had an underground worker as an escort. One of them described the loading.

"Imagine a dark night and a lonesome corner of a small town," he related. "The dirty little streets are unlighted. One sees no living soul as one drives into the town. Our three big trucks turn into a courtyard. I follow in a small car. In the courtyard one sees nothing, hears nothing.

"But when I get out of my car I see a long line of people, like shadows along the wall. They stand in silence, their baggage already on their backs, their backs bowed. It is a few minutes past one in the morning, and at a signal from a man at the head of the line the people begin to climb on the trucks one by one, like soldiers on the eve of an invasion.

"I stand by the trucks and watch a group of women and children climb on the trucks, children without mothers, mothers without children. I look on and see *tayere yunge yiddishe ponimer* [dear young Jewish faces]. There are packs on their backs and a hot fire in their eyes. Some smile. Others cry with joy. Some hug and kiss each other and hold hands. Nobody says a word. I ask a small girl near me—it is a cold night, with rain and a chilling wind—'Are you cold?' She answers in a whisper, 'How can I be cold on a night like this?' "

As the ship filled up, the atmosphere became hilarious. Some of the younger children were exploring the ship, clambering all over the place, as excited as any group of youngsters on shipboard for the first time.

The older orthodox men began promenading the deck for a *shpatsir* [promenade] in black vests and *yarmilkes* [skull caps]. In the galley, hefty volunteers from among the refugees had set to work with housewifely zest.

Our passengers wore clothes which might have been the leavings of several dozen secondhand shops on Delancey Street. The men wore everything from baggy

knickers to overalls. Many of the women had peasant ker-
chiefs over their heads.

The last to come aboard was Victor Baumgard, a stocky
twenty-nine-year old Belgian from Arras. It had taken
almost six hours to load our passengers. There were a
thousand and fifteen in all. I stood at the head of the gangplank and helped every one of them aboard.

Finally the moment came when we cast off the ropes
and waved good-by to the *Haganah* workers on shore.

All the refugees were ordered below decks as we prepared to make for the open sea. We did not want to arouse
the curiosity of too many people on other boats and on
shore. A pilot boat came alongside and slowly took us out
to sea. A few minutes before six we dropped the pilot and
headed south in the driving wind and rain.

Down below, the people were packed in like the cargo
of an African slaver. At six-thirty, when we could see
nothing but the highest mountains on the horizon and
there were no other boats in sight, the captain blew a
whistle as signal that the people could come up from
below. The *shomrim* spread the news and our passengers
streamed out on deck to look with wonder on that great sea.
For them it was the sea which washes the shores of *Eretz,*
whither they were bound.

IV

Among our refugees were five Gentiles who intended to settle in Palestine, four for religious, one for idealistic reasons.

Two-thirds of the refugees were men, for more men than women survived the Nazi terror. Most of our passengers were thirty years of age or younger. Only a hundred and ninety-six were over thirty. There were a few couples who had married in DP camps since the liberation. Except for the Polish Jews who had lived in the Soviet Union during the war and brought out their families under the Russo-Polish repatriation agreement, the refugees were all remnants of families.

Our oldest passenger was seventy-eight; our youngest, ten. The seventy-eight-year-old was a tall Russian *subbotnik,* a kind of Russian Seventh Day Adventist. He and his family had been converted to Judaism. He wore a black skull cap. His long head, grave eyes, and bearded face reminded one of the pictures of Anatole France in his old age. He was traveling with his wife, their son and Gentile-Polish daughter-in-law.

The son spoke fluent Yiddish as well as Hebrew. He was a *Chassid,* and with his sparse, sandy beard and flowing ear locks looked like a typical member of that pietistic Jewish sect. He said that his two brothers, who also intended to settle in Palestine, were studying at a Jewish theological seminary which had been established since the liberation in Frankfurt. One brother intended to become a rabbi, the other a *shoykhet,* an orthodox slaughterer.

Our other non-Jewish passenger was a twenty-four-year-old French girl from Grenoble, a shy, slight, quiet person. Her father was a gentleman farmer. During the war she worked in the French resistance. There she first met Jews in helping some of them escape deportation to Germany. She got to know several of the Jewish resistance leaders and became interested in Zionism. When I asked her why she was going to Palestine, she said she felt that she could best lead a truly socialist life by entering one of the Jewish collective settlements in the Holy Land.

Our ten-year-old was a dark-haired Polish-Jewish girl named Judith Greenberg. She was clever, sharp-tongued, and precocious, and wrote poetry in Polish. After her parents had been sent to their deaths at Treblinka, her aunt had escaped with her from the Warsaw ghetto and, giving her the name of Szofel, had placed her in a Polish orphan home as a Christian child. The aunt had lived with false Aryan papers as a Polish slave laborer in Germany, and had come back for her after the liberation.

"That child," the woman told me proudly, "has crossed five borders illegally on her way to this ship."

With them was the woman's husband, a broad-shouldered man of medium height who had been in the Polish Army in 1939, in a Russian camp as a prisoner of war, and in the Polish Army again until the end of the war.

There were Jews from sixteen different countries on board, including one rather lonely Egyptian Jew who spoke only his native Arabic and a smattering of French. He had gone to Italy as a laborer before the war and been deported to a German concentration camp as a "non-Aryan."

There were five hundred and eighty-five refugees from Poland. The next largest national group, a hundred and nine, were Czechoslovakian Jews, most of them from Slovakia and Carpatho-Russia. There were eighty-four immigrants from Holland, all young people. Some of them were German and Austrian Jews who had gone to Holland before the war to escape Nazi persecution. But many were Dutch, members of families which had settled in Holland in the sixteenth century after the exodus from Spain.

The Dutch youngsters looked like illustrations from *Hans Brinker and the Silver Skates*. Their parents had been deported to Germany and killed by the Nazis. They were not fleeing Holland—they were going to Palestine. They spoke of their native land with sad affection, but they were *khalutsim,* Zionist pioneers bent on building a Jewish homeland. English rather than Yiddish was their secondary language.

One of them, a plump, rosy girl of twenty-two, expressed the nationalist awakening which was sending these youngsters to a new and difficult country in a kind of fierce, proud reaction to the events of the Hitler period. She too had lost her parents to the Germans.

"I never was a Jew before the war. But now that six million Jews have been killed, I will be a Jew too," she said with an air of cheerfully stubborn defiance.

There was a lovely girl in the group from Holland, a

tall, graceful Viennese named Ilse Walter. She was twenty-six and had intended to be a chemist. She had fled to Holland under false papers when the Nazis occupied Austria and had remained there throughout the occupation. Part of the time she lived in hiding in the home of the present Dutch Minister of Agriculture. He was an underground leader and sheltered many fugitives, including political prisoners, escaped prisoners of war, Jews, and British Intelligence agents. Later she worked as a nurse in an Old Peoples' Home in Amsterdam, where only the Dutch director knew she was Jewish. So far as she knew, her whole family had been killed except for an uncle, who before the war had settled in Palestine, and possibly her father, who had escaped from a German concentration camp into Russia before the Nazi attack on the Soviet Union.

There were fifty-nine Jews from Hungary, fifty-one from Rumania, forty-four from Germany. Twenty-four were from Lithuania. Twenty were from France, twelve from Belgium, and eleven from Austria. There were six Russian Jews, three Latvians, two Swiss, two Turkish, two Greek, and the Egyptian. One of the Latvian Jews had settled in Palestine before the war and gone back to Riga in 1939 to see his parents. He had been there when the war began.

Linguistically, the ship was a floating Babel. Yiddish varies considerably from country to country and there were about a dozen different dialects aboard. Even from those countries in which Yiddish was the common language of the Jews, there were many who had been completely assimilated and spoke only the native language of their birthplaces.

The two Turks spoke *Ladino,* the Mediterranean and Levantine counterpart of Yiddish spoken by descendants of Spanish Jews scattered by the Inquisition. It is mixed Spanish and Hebrew, as Yiddish is basically mixed German and Hebrew. The Greeks, a man and his wife who married in Paris after the liberation, spoke only Greek and French. The husband was the tallest man on board, a man who might have served as a model for Praxiteles. He was deported from Greece to a German concentration camp in 1942. Everyone was curious to know his occupation. When I asked him he said he was a pastry cook.

One hundred and thirty-eight persons on board had no party affiliation. The rest belonged to seventeen different Zionist parties, the largest group being orthodox. There were one hundred and ninety-five members of *Agudath Israel* and ninety of *Poale Mizrachi* [orthodox labor]. Next were a hundred and forty revisionists, chauvinistic and right wing. There were eighty-two *khalutsim* from the *Hashomer Hatzair,* a left-wing socialist group which advocates a bi-nationalist Arab-Jewish Palestine rather than a Jewish state.

Of the thousand and fifteen passengers, five hundred and sixty-eight were *khalutsim* who intended to spend their lives in collective settlements in Palestine. All of them were socialists of one kind or another.

V

More than three hundred of the refugees had served during the war in the Red Army, the Polish Army, the Czech Army, or with the Partisans.

The youngest of these war veterans was a boy of thirteen. His name was Hersh Arbas and he came from Warsaw. He was a cute little fellow and allowed the run of the bridge as a special pet of the captain and the crew. He wanted some day to be a sailor. He was the youngest of three small boys in berets on board, all three of them as agile and noisy as monkeys. They had an uproarious time during the voyage, playing hide-and-go-seek around the decks and climbing up and down the rigging. Hersh was the envy of his two friends because he had carried a revolver and lived and fought with a group of Polish Partisans.

Hersh's father had been a wealthy man, and he had sufficient means to buy safety for several years. From 1939 to 1942 he lived hidden in a Polish farmhouse with his father, mother, and small sister. In 1942 there was a raid on the farmhouse and the Germans took his parents away. He never saw them again. Hersh and his four-year-old sister remained in hiding with the farmer, who had been paid by Hersh's father to take care of them. But one day Hersh saw police coming to the farmhouse and concluded that they had been betrayed.

"I grabbed my sister by the hand," Hersh told us, "and we ran out the back door toward a nearby forest. The police saw us and opened fire. One shot killed my sister but I got away. I hid in the woods by day and traveled by night, and managed to reach the ghetto in Krosnick. I'd only been there a few weeks when the Germans rounded up thirty of us, mostly older people, and put us on a death wagon for the crematorium.

"On the way, when it got dark, one of the older men threw me over the side of the wagon into a ditch and jumped in after me. We stayed there until the wagon was out of sight. We wandered around for twelve days. A party of German soldiers caught sight of us from a distance and opened fire, killing the man with me. A truck loaded with flour was passing at the time, and I jumped on the back of it and got away. There were nails on the road put there by Partisans to sabotage traffic. When a tire blew out and the driver stopped the truck to fix it, Partisans hiding along the road killed him.

"The Partisans were friendly. They instructed me to use a false Polish name and left me with a rich peasant. I stayed with him for eight months until he began to suspect that I was a Jew. I fled to a small town. The town was surrounded by the Germans several nights later in an effort to capture Partisans hiding out in it. There was heavy fighting in the raid. I don't know what happened to me, but I woke up to find myself with a bandaged head in a forest hideout with a group of Partisans."

Hersh remained with these Partisans until the area in

which they operated was liberated by the Russians in 1945. They gave him a Russian revolver.

"Yah!" he said with a broad smile when I asked him if he ever used it.

The Partisans were Poles, except for their captain and their doctor, who were both Russians. These two were the only ones who knew that he was Jewish. After the liberation the Partisan captain placed Hersh in a Jewish children's home run by the orthodox *Agudath Israel.*

There were experienced military men among us who had been tailors, storekeepers, weavers, locksmiths, and woodworkers in the ghettoes of Poland before the war. I talked with one who had been a locksmith in Pinsk.

When the Russians occupied that part of Poland in 1939 he was drafted into the Red Army and sent to an officers' school in Leningrad where he became a tank specialist with the rank of lieutenant. He fought all through the siege of Leningrad and was later assigned to the Polish forces and participated in the liberation of Warsaw.

A carpenter from Pinsk had become a Partisan commander. His band worked in close contact with the Red Army and he was awarded a Stalin medal after the liberation.

A Jew from Lodz had had a varied career as an artillery officer. He fought in the Polish Army in 1939, was captured by the Russians when they invaded Poland and held a prisoner of war until 1941. When the Nazi invasion began he volunteered for the Red Army. He served eight months in the Russian Army and then three and a half years in the Polish Army. When the war ended he did not wait to be demobilized. He took advantage of a fourteen-day leave to escape across the Czech border. There was nothing to keep him in Poland, he said; all his relatives were dead and the Polish Army very anti-Semitic.

Some of the Jews had survived in peculiar ways. With us was a Polish Jew from Cracow who had owned a large printing establishment before the war. He was sent to Auschwitz, but soon found himself transferred on a strange assignment.

"Several other Jews and I were summoned to the camp headquarters one day," he related, "and told to make ready for a journey. We were taken to a concentration camp at Sachshausen near Berlin. Sachshausen was a camp for political prisoners. This fact was known abroad and the camp was never bombed.

"We were placed in a special underground section of the camp from which even SS men were barred. There were one hundred and forty of us there—all printers and all Jews, from France, Italy, and Czechoslovakia as well as from Poland. Except for the fact that we were kept closely confined we were well treated and well fed. We were put to work counterfeiting foreign currency and foreign documents for the Gestapo."

This man told me an incredible story. He said he had once been congratulated on his birthday by Heinrich Himmler, the head of the Gestapo.

"It was in 1944," he told me. "I was foreman on the night shift and the workers under me had planned a little celebration for my birthday. That night Himmler came to visit the counterfeiting plant. With him was the Nazi

leader Kaltenbrunner. You must understand that we were
a favored group, treated well and never beaten. Himmler
was very pleased with the work we were turning out, and
when he came in and saw some birthday decorations on
the wall he asked whose birthday it was. 'Let him stand
forth,' Himmler ordered. When I walked up to him and
saluted, he asked: 'Who are you?'

" 'I'm a Polish Jew," Herr Commisar,' I said.

"Himmler shook hands with me and wished me a happy
birthday. He said he was pleased with the work my shift
was doing and asked what I would like for my birthday.
I was taken aback by his friendliness, and I still don't
know how I had the courage to do it, but I pointed to a
paper placard put up on the wall for the birthday party
which had one word on it—*Freiheit*.

" 'Only that,' I said, my knees a little shaky.

"Himmler answered with an odd smile, *'Es kommt'* [It
is coming]. I don't suppose the freedom he meant was
more than the 'freedom' which came to those of our comrades who fell ill and were taken away never to reappear.
None of us who worked there was ever intended to know
freedom again except in the other world. But freedom was
coming all the same, and I was permitted to see it."

I can't vouch for this story. All I can report is that it
was told me in a matter-of-fact way one morning by a man
who did not seem to be lying. When I asked him what
happened after that, he added a detail of a kind that made
me think his story was authentic. He said Himmler ordered
one of the guards to give the printer a special issue of
a hundred and thirty cigarettes for his birthday. The odd,

exact number and the anti-climactic detail seemed to me
the kind of thing one does not fabricate. I think a Mun-
chausen would have thought of a more dramatic climax.

VI

There was a man on board whom we all called Rudy
and a girl I shall call Ruth. Theirs was the most exciting
story I heard on my trip. In some ways it was a horrible
story.

When I heard it I kept thinking of a famous Latin
saying whose source I have forgotten, *"Homo homini
lupus."* This is usually translated "man preys on man"
but literally it means, "man is a wolf to man."

The story is the more dreadful because the hero, Rudy,
was himself part wolf. It was this streak of fierce and
predatory criminality that made it possible for him to survive and to help others to survive.

The story of Rudy and Ruth has elements of beauty as
well as horror, for it is a story of courage in the face of
terror, degradation, loneliness, and death.

I spoke of having heard this story. Actually I had to
piece it together, to draw it out bit by bit in the course of
several talks. I have added nothing to it. It is too melodramatic to need any gloss of the fictional, and this glimpse
of human beings in hell is too memorable for anything
but the truth.

Rudy was not the real name of the hero. I do not know his real name, nor would I print it if I did, for he was one of the leading figures of the underground which has been rescuing Jews from Europe since the beginning of the Hitler period. Ruth was only one of many hundreds whom he saved.

Ruth was a *khalutsa,* a pioneer in Zion, a member of the left-wing *Hashomir Hatzair* or Young Guard, a Marxist Zionist group.

Ruth was twenty. Rudy was in his fifties. I first met him on the seacoast of a European country bordering the Mediterranean. He was described as the foremost character among the refugees there, a Jew whom the others called *Shimshon Ha-Giboor,* or Samson the hero. The Hebrew is that applied to the original Samson in the Bible.

He was an ox of a man, a sort of Jewish Man Mountain Dean, with big brown eyes and a short brown beard. He had the hoarse, rasping voice of a man accustomed to shouting orders at crowds.

We did not become friends at once. Rudy shied away from me when he was told that I was an American newspaperman. There was very little that could frighten Rudy, but he looked scared when I took out my notebook and pencil while talking with him.

There was always a little knot of curious admirers and hangers-on around Rudy.

He called me aside—that first day I met him ashore—and, in as close to a whisper as that bull's voice of his would allow, asked: "Are you going with us on the boat to *Eretz?*"

He eyed me shrewdly, like one not accustomed to being deceived. I was under strict orders to tell no one that I was going to travel the underground route to Palestine. I shrugged my shoulders as though the thought had never occurred to me, and said I didn't know. Rudy looked down at me for a moment, then with a satisfied grin slapped me heartily on the back.

"We'll talk on the boat," he said, "but not one word now. If a word gets out to the papers before I leave . . ." he made a quick motion with his big hand across his thick throat.

Some of the things I heard about Rudy were so incredible that I checked his story with friends in the underground. They were a sober little band, too genuinely heroic themselves for heroics and much too busy to brag. They vouched for him.

Rudy was a Polish Jew who had been orphaned at the age of eight. He was then twice as big and strong as any boy his age. He made his way to Cuba before the First World War and grew up in the streets of Havana. After the war he became a rum runner and served a term in a U. S. Federal penitentiary where he made friends with a well-known American gangster—not a man of Capone's structure but an important man in the business.

Rudy went back to rum running after his release from prison. When the repeal of prohibition ended that occupation, he became a professional wrestler, and later a strong man in a circus. He was in Europe on tour with a circus in 1939 and the war caught him in Poland.

Rudy was captured by the Nazis and sent to a concentration camp as a Jew. There his size and strength attracted attention; the Germans used him constantly, as they might a fine farm animal, for blood transfusions. I do not know all that happened to him. He said once that it would take a whole book to tell his life adequately. I know that he turned up a couple of years later in the camp at Auschwitz, notorious for its cruelty and crematoriums. It was there that the adventure of Rudy and Ruth took place.

I first met Ruth on board the boat our second night out. I was wandering around the deck, talking to as many people as I could and soaking it all in—the starry sky, the lonely Mediterranean, the happy singing, the crowds of Jews milling about on deck as they might on Delancey Street or Petticoat Lane. Then I saw a girl who looked very sick sitting on the deck with her back against the superstructure amidships. (I hope that's the proper nautical way to say it.)

I asked if I could help her, but she only smiled wanly, pointed to her stomach and said she'd be all right. She looked as though company was the last thing in the world she wanted. I went away. The next night she looked much better. I asked her how she felt and struck up a conversation.

She was a Polish Jew of a rather well-to-do family. Like most people on that boat, she had lost her family in concentration camp and crematorium. She, too, had been at Auschwitz, under sentence of death as a political prisoner.

"Have you noticed that big fellow on deck?" she asked. She did not call him Rudy but used another name,

which I presume is his real one. I knew at once whom
she meant. I nodded.

"I never expected to see him alive again," she said. "He
saved my life at Auschwitz. I never did know what happened to him afterward until I met him again on this
boat."

Ruth was not a glamour girl. In the first place she was
fat, not obesely broad-beamed like so many of the women
on board, but certainly plump. Perhaps the plumpness was,
in part, occupational. For Ruth had been studying a practical trade which would be useful in a collective settlement in Palestine. She chose to be a dairy maid, and after
years of Nazi concentration fare she loved nothing better
than bread and milk. She admitted that she had indulged
in this liking every few hours while working as a milk-
maid, and the result was to obliterate any possible re-
semblance she might once have had to a pretty girl.

Secondly, Ruth never combed her hair. It was a wild,
unruly mop of black curls that she brushed back with her
hands, or blew back with protruding lower lip, when it
got in her eyes which were blue and beautiful, or when
it interfered with her conversation, which was brilliant,
and—when she found somebody she liked—unending, as
if to make up for years of silence.

As a pioneer woman-to-be she affected to despise femi-
nine graces. She loved to tell how her incorrigible milk-
maid manners had shocked a wealthy and sophisticated
aunt in Brussels who had tried to dissuade her from going
to Palestine and to make her into a leisured lady.

Her favorite costume consisted of dungarees, for which

Nature had not entirely suited her, and a leather zipper jacket, which she wore with a swagger. She never used rouge or lipstick, but her rosy cheeks and creamy skin needed neither. Despite her contempt for femininity she was something of a charmer, a bit of a flirt, and after the first few nights always had a fascinated coterie of boys from the crew and the *khalutsim* around her. She was witty, vivacious, a born raconteur. She was no rapt-eyed listener. The boys could hardly get a word in edgewise, but they found her enchanting. So did I.

The most amazing thing about Ruth was the wholesomeness and naiveté with which she had emerged from her concentration camp experiences. She was a child, but an extraordinarily perceptive one. She was very quick to understand the essential qualities of the people she met on shipboard, as I knew from her reactions to the various members of the crew, whom I had known longer and more intimately than she had. I called her "wonder child" or "young cow," depending on how I felt about her at the moment. She was both. She was widely read and could describe her past experiences with a vividness that made me encourage her to write.

The first night we really talked we stood by the rail watching the phosphorescent glow of the waves breaking against the ship, and looking at the stars.

"You can't imagine what life was like in a concentration camp," Ruth said. She pointed to the stars. "It's as if I were to come down from one of the planets and tried to explain what life was like in another world. Even now, a year after the liberation, I find it hard to believe some of the things that happened to me and to other people. To see people around you beaten, hanged, and shot as part of what was a normal round, always to expect the same fate yourself tomorrow, that was our daily life."

That night she described her feelings the night before her scheduled execution at Auschwitz.

"I was in a bunker, a prison half underground, with a small window near the top of the wall. I stood all that night on a box, looking out at the stars. Around camp-fires outside, gypsies were waiting for the wagons which would take them to the gas chambers and the crematorium. I have never seen such beautiful creatures, men and women with black eyes and the handsome swarthy faces of free wild creatures. They were very friendly to us in the camp because they shared with the Jews the brunt of the Nazi extermination campaign. They were very brave. I cried for them and for their courage, not for myself. That I was to be executed was something I could not really grasp.

"I felt my hand and said to myself, 'This is my hand,' and I felt my face and said 'This is my face,' I felt my head and said 'This is my head, and tomorrow all this that is me will exist no longer because somebody wills it so'."

But Ruth did not die that next day. Her life was spared by reason of the strange ascendancy which Rudy, a Jew, had managed to achieve in the camp.

Rudy's rise began with a hundred and twenty lashes he received the day he entered Auschwitz. He had been caught near a frontier town and was rightly suspected of working in what the Germans felt was the beginning of a Jewish underground rescue organization. He denied any such connections; the lashes were intended to make him talk. Fifty were enough to wreck an ordinary man and Rudy did gratefully lapse into unconsciousness long before he had taken the full hundred and twenty. They were administered by two men who stood on either side of him and brought their bullwhips down alternately on his naked back.

"I wouldn't give those bastards the satisfaction of hearing a Jew cry out," Rudy said, "and I bit hard on my tongue to keep silent before I passed out. It took me several weeks to recover from that beating, but I never told them what they wanted to know. The beating had one strange result. The SS camp commander saw me undergo what no ordinary person could have survived, and in his own way he took a liking to me.

"He was a tall man, very thin, and he loved cruelty. He is still alive somewhere in Germany—in fact some months ago I heard that he was trying to reach me to testify on his behalf to Allied War Crimes investigators."

I felt that Rudy rather liked the fellow.

The SS camp commander made Rudy a *Kapo* and later promoted him to be chief *Kapo* for one whole section of Auschwitz. The word *Kapo* is German, an abbreviated form for *KZ Polizei* [concentration camp police]. *Kapo*s were chosen from among the inmates, Jewish *Kapo*s from the Jews, Polish *Kapo*s from the Poles. Besides keeping order, they did the dirty work of the Nazis, beating their own people, spying upon them, and currying favor with the

Nazis at the expense of their fellows. But a few used their influence to help their own people. A few were heroes who worked with the underground under the very noses of their Nazi masters to help others escape. Rudy was one of these.

As head *Kapo* Rudy was not without means, if he had the resourcefulness to use them and the nerve to risk death in doing so. For one thing there was a closely guarded storeroom at Auschwitz where the Nazis kept gold, jewelry, money, and other valuable taken from Jews who had been sent to be gassed and burned. SS men were denied access to this room. The valuables were the property of the state. The storeroom was guarded by Jews; every few months the guards would be sent to the crematorium and new ones would be assigned their places. For a Jew to be caught in the camp with valuables of this kind meant instant death. Rudy risked it.

Rudy organized a kind of black market at Auschwitz which dealt in everything, including human beings. He bribed guards with cigarettes, brandy, meat, and luxuries to establish underground connections between the various camps for rescue work. As his reputation grew, Rudy found that he had another source of funds. Those Jews who had managed to conceal some valuables up to the very doors of the gas chambers turned these over to the Jews who drove the death wagons, asking that they be handed over to Rudy. The drivers usually did so out of fear of what would happen to them if such things were found in their possession when they got back to camp.

As Rudy grew bolder he brought the SS commander under his influence.

"I had a jeweler in the camp," Rudy told me, "make up a gold ring with two diamonds from the storehouse. I took it to the SS commander, clicked my heels, saluted, and said, 'Herr Oberkommandant, I found this' and handed him the diamond ring. He looked me in the eye and said, 'What do you mean by saying you found this?' I repeated that I had found it. He asked, 'Why didn't you take it to the chief of your section? Why did you bring it to me?' I kept a straight face and answered, 'I didn't think I had to take it to him. I thought you might like to have it.' He grabbed me by the shoulders and peered full into my face for several minutes. But he finally took the ring. He knew, from those hundred and twenty lashes, that I was a man who could keep my mouth shut. From that time on a new relationship developed between us.

"He liked women and I found out that he was keeping several in Germany. He needed money. I saw to it that he was well supplied. Every week I would slip out a bit of jewelry he could send to a girl friend, or smuggle out a bit of gold for him. He began to depend on me and when I needed a favor I could usually get it from him. All this was very valuable for the underground. We weren't able to do very much, but that little was precious."

One of the things he had been able to do was to save Ruth. Ruth was caught in Vienna after leaving Poland in 1942 with false Aryan papers. She had been asked by a friend to carry a message. She did not know what the message was, all she knew was that it had something to do with an illegal organization. She asked no questions, for the less information one had the less there was to tell under torture. She was accused of being a communist underground worker, sentenced to death by hanging, and shipped to Auschwitz for execution. I tell it quickly here, and Ruth told it quickly to me, but I gathered there were many days of questioning in Vienna and that the methods used were not pleasant to recall.

"I had never been in a concentration camp before," Ruth said. "When I got to Auschwitz I was put into a big bunker with two hundred other girls. The others were all Polish and some were very unfriendly. They found out I was a Jew and there were many gibes at my expense. I didn't expect to live, but I was determined to show them how a Jew could die.

"One of the Polish girls mocked, 'So you're a Jew, are you? Well, I guess Rudy will try to help you. He's always doing things for Jews.' I didn't know who Rudy was and when he appeared the next day I didn't like him. He said he would try to help me, but I felt that I was beyond help. I thought he was just a big talker. I was preparing myself to die bravely and I didn't want to be bothered by false hopes.

"Rudy came back the next day and brought me a pretty dress. I had nothing to wear so I put it on, and I was foolish enough to feel pleased. I didn't realize then that he got the dress by taking it from a body in the gas chamber. I didn't know yet that in a concentration camp every breath one drew was at somebody else's expense."

Rudy interrupted to tell me how he felt when he first saw Ruth.

"Ha!" Rudy said, "she was stubborn and unfriendly.

But when I first set eyes on her I loved her as if she were my own daughter. She was such a sweet child. I couldn't let her go to her death. I had to find some way to save her."

"I knew Ruth was supposed to be hanged the next morning," Rudy went on. "I had very little time to lose. I got to my friend the commander at about two in the morning. I brought with me a bottle of the best *schnapps* I had. The commander was a great drinker. I never met another man with his capacity. I fed him the *schnapps* and gave him a shave. He liked me to shave him. By the time I was through there was a great deal of *schnapps* under his belt and he was in a cheerful mood. He pinched my cheek and said, 'Well, Rudy my boy, what can I do for you?' I said, 'Herr Oberkommandant, I have a favor to ask that means a great deal to me.' He said, 'If it's anything within reason you shall have it.'

" 'You know that Jewish girl in the Polish bunker," I said. He looked serious at once. I said, 'I'm in love with that girl and I must have her. Give me her life.'

"The commander screamed at me, 'Rudy, you're crazy. That's impossible. She's no ordinary Jew you can spirit away. She's a traitor to the state. There's a whole carload full of documents on her. This is too big. I can't do anything'."

Rudy played his last card. He knew how dependent the commander had grown on the money and jewels Rudy brought him.

"I said to him, 'Herr Oberkommandant, if that girl dies I die too. I can't live without her. If she hangs tomorrow I'll take my life the same day.'

"The SS commander looked at me with fury in his eyes. I looked straight back at him without dropping mine. I tried to look calm, but I didn't feel calm. I felt my knees would give way as I waited for his decision. The next few minutes were the most anxious I've ever spent.

"Finally the commander shouted at me, 'You crazy Jew, how can such a thing be done?' Then I knew I had won. I had a plan ready and while he blustered and raged I explained it to him."

There had to be a body. A death certificate had to be sent to higher authorities. The means by which a substitute body and a false certificate may be obtained are too dreadful to relate. But before dawn that morning false Aryan papers had been made out for Ruth and she was sent under special guard to a labor camp for Polish girls.

Almost the first question Ruth asked Rudy when they met on the boat was, "Whatever happened to your Czech friend?"

One day the SS brought a prisoner to Auschwitz who was a Czech army officer. He was a Jew and Rudy took an instant liking to him.

"He was a man," Rudy said with emphasis. "He had blue eyes that were afraid of nothing. He carried himself like a true soldier, and he treated his SS captors with calm contempt. I loved him," said Rudy, pounding his big fist against his heart, "and I wanted to help him get away."

Ruth told me the story as she had seen and heard it from the prison.

"I first heard about the officer from Rudy on one of his visits to me," she related. "I wasn't surprised a few days

later to hear that the Czech had escaped. I was amused
to learn that after the escape Rudy had stormed up and
down the camp making the most bloody threats as to what
he would do to that cursed Jew if he were ever recaptured.
'I'll flog him to death with my own hands!' Rudy had
cried. But that night he came to me and danced up and
down with joy as he told me of the escape.

"Unfortunately the Czech was recaptured about a week
later. He was sentenced to be hanged. The SS authorities
suspected that Rudy had had a hand in the escape and
planned to punish him too. Ordinarily Jews were hanged
by Poles and Poles by Jews as part of a deliberate plan
to make the two peoples hate each other more. But on
this occasion Rudy was ordered to hang his friend with
his own hands."

"I almost went crazy," Rudy broke in. "I didn't know
what to do. I went to the leaders of the Jews in the camp
and asked them to advise me. They said, 'Rudy, nothing
can help that man. He must die. If you try to interfere
you will lose your life, too, and you are the only person
here who can help us a little. The man must die and you
must obey the authorities and hang him'."

Ruth recalled how that Czech Jew looked the morning
set for the execution.

"I saw him go marching proudly past my bunker, his
head erect. He stopped and threw me a kiss. He knew of
me through Rudy, and his eyes said a beautiful farewell."

When the Czech came with his hands bound and his
mouth gagged to the scaffold, he looked Rudy in the eye
"as though trying to tell me not to be afraid, that he

understood, that he did not blame me, that we were still good friends and to go ahead."

But Rudy had already made up his mind to risk everything rather than hang his friend.

"I always carried a razor blade hidden on me for use as a kind of last resort," he said. "Shortly before the hanging was to take place I took my razor blade and cut into both sides of that rope, just enough for my purpose. When I put the noose around his neck and pulled the lever that opened the trap door he dropped, but it was the rope that broke, not his neck. The Germans took him away to another camp. They ordered me hanged in his place. But my friend the SS commander saved me. He insisted that the fault lay with the rope and not me, and demanded that he be allowed to test a length of the same rope. But in the test he used a section of iron rail so heavy that it broke the rope. The commander claimed that this showed that I was the innocent victim and that the rope had been rotten."

I asked Rudy what happened afterwards to the Czech officer.

"I don't know," he said sadly. "I assume he was executed. I never heard from him again."

VII

The first part of our trip to Palestine took eight days. It was uneventful and happy, despite the discomforts.

The discomforts had largely to do with our sleeping arrangements. The low, narrow wooden bunks were of a kind on which only the young, healthy, and dog-tired could find rest. The few mattresses were reserved for the sick. The rest lay down in their clothes or spread blankets on the splintery, unfinished lumber.

There was little ventilation below deck and at night the air grew stale and stinking. Bare feet stuck out from the bunks into the passageways. The silence was broken by coughing, the sighs of the sleepless, and the moans of the sick. Sleepy-eyed young *shomrim* stood or sat on watch all night at the gangways below deck. The real heroes were the weary members of the sanitation squad who came running with buckets and mops whenever the seasick were too ill to go on deck. Each case would set off others unless and until there was a quick cleanup.

A corps of two dozen boys and girls with red *Mogen Dovid* armbands who had been given a course in first aid brought lemons and wet compresses for the seasick, comforted the frightened, slapped the occasional hysteric, and gave injections in a few cases of heart disease. One of the nurses was a big Hungarian girl who was stronger than most of the men on board. She was very proud of the American slang she had picked up. She had the right combination of tenderness, roughness, and strength for a good nurse. It was one of the memorable sights of the voyage to see her grab a sick man around the neck, open his mouth and force a spoonful of unpleasant medicine down his throat. With her big arms, black eyes and dark skin she looked like a young gypsy matriarch.

The seriously ill were taken to the doctor's office, a small room below deck which was normally used as the officers' mess. But on this voyage the officers ate with the crew and the mess had been fitted up with two bunks for the doctor and his wife. A big makeshift cabinet held a small crateload of medicines and instruments.

The doctor was one of our illegal immigrants. He was a slight man of middle height who had been born in Bukovina but lived in France since the first World War. His black-haired, vivacious wife was a French Jew, and their little cabin was the social center for our French colony. The French and Belgian youngsters foregathered there and the cabin was always full of French conversation and French songs. The doctor had worked with the Maquis during the war. He was an idealist. He said he did not wish to practice in the cities but to become the doctor member of one of the new collective settlements.

Of course, the news that there was a *Herr Doktor* aboard, and that his services were free, enthralled the hypochondriacs. There were always women in his cabin, crying in Yiddish, "Oh, Doctor, I'm dying . . . I'm fainting. . . . Oh, Doctor, I'll never get to Palestine."

The doctor was a cultured man and enjoyed talking about books and politics. When interrupted by one of these grave cases he was likely to shout unfeelingly:

"Nothing is going to happen to you. You're not going to die."

He would give these "sick" a couple of sugar pills or a slice of lemon, and sometimes add in an exasperated aside to me, intended for the ears of the sick one:

"What's she bothering me for? She's as healthy as a horse."

The hypochondriacs were convinced that the doctor was a monster.

After two days of stormy weather, we came into calm and sunny seas. The most determined hypochondriacs succumbed to the restful beauty of the Mediterranean, the languorous days and starry nights. Even the woman we called the Sleeping Beauty gave in to the fine weather after three days and sat up.

For four days she had lain, wrapped in a blanket on top of a life raft on the forward deck, just in front of and below the bridge. She was the most beautiful woman on board, a graceful lovely creature of twenty. Her husband, a handsome Polish engineer in his late thirties, led a miserable life putting compresses on her head, helping her when she vomited, and coaxing her to take a little food. We learned that she was four months with child.

The Sleeping Beauty and her husband had a very romantic story. They lived and worked as Aryans under the Germans. They met and fell in love. Each discovered that the other was Jewish. They had married after the liberation. She was the engineer's second wife. He had lost his first family.

Whenever we sighted another ship our passengers were quickly herded below lest our crowded decks arouse suspicion. Each time that happened, the decks were washed and swept. These periods below and the nights were the worst for our people. There was a curfew at eleven o'clock

when all the passengers had to go to bed. They began to
come up again before dawn.

The food was not too bad, but neither was it too plentiful. There was plenty of bread, which I thought delicious,
although our four refugee bakers complained and apolo-
gized every day about the inadequate oven. The meals consisted largely of a combination stew and soup for the
non-kosher and a thick vegetable soup for the kosher.
There was little coffee or tea except for the crew, the
nurses, and the men of the sanitary squad. Perhaps the
man who suffered most from the meals was our chief cook,
an American *khaluts,* who worried constantly that he
wasn't able to serve quite enough. He grew so melancholy
that the crew stopped kidding him about his cooking,
which had been one of our favorite occupations at mess.

Early in the morning the orthodox began to come out
on deck to pray, putting on their prayer shawls and phylac-
teries and bowing energetically toward the east.

Breakfast was served at about seven, most people eating
on deck. The passengers organized themselves into groups,
and each group leader with a helper brought up the food
in buckets, with paper dishes and fresh loaves of bread.
Cigarettes and chocolate were given out several times during the voyage. There was powdered milk for those who
needed it. Lunch was served at noon and dinner at six.

Despite the discomforts and shortcomings, there never
was a gayer ship on the high seas. Our decks looked like
Orchard Beach or Coney Island on a hot Sunday. They
were packed with people in every possible costume, from

bathing suits to the black mohair vests of the shirt-sleeved older orthodox men.

Below us one day three caps and one *yarmilke* were eating hardtack smeared with butter while they carried on a voluble conversation. A girl played a concertina on top of a pile of life rafts, surrounded by admirers. A fat red-head with a purple hair ribbon sat by herself on a hatch, happily singing a Hebrew song and rocking back and forth to the rhythm. Two lovesick calves held hands as they sat along the rail: she plump, he thin with horn-rimmed spectacles. They kissed soulfully. An unshaven little man with a red Turkish cap wandered around in search of something, looking like an organ grinder's lost monkey.

Big, fat Rudy, the ex-circus strong man, dressed only in white shorts with a towel wrapped around his head like a turban, sat on a ventilator, swarthy, fierce, and bearded as a wild Mongol chief or galley slavemaster. A group of *khalutsim* were dancing the Palestinian *hora,* holding hands in a great moving circle as they leaped and sang.

The first mate sat on the railing of the bridge, contentedly smoking a cigar as he looked on.

"Yes," he said, as if after profound reflection, "it's the old Hudson River Day Line all over again—next stop, Bear Mountain."

VIII

So little happened during the first week of our journey that we were completely unprepared for the dangers and hardships which were to arise on our way through the blockaded waters of Palestine. Our ship could have made the entire trip in four days and our slow progress puzzled us. But since the trip was pleasant we paid scant attention to the leisurely pace. The reason for our loitering was soon to become apparent.

During that first week on board, a ship's paper would have been hard put for news. I spent my time talking with the passengers. There was hardly one aboard whose life would not have made an exciting story. That week on the Mediterranean was the first peaceful interlude they had enjoyed in years.

There was a bit of excitement the third day out when two long-lost cousins met each other on the foreward deck with shouts of joy, hugs, and kisses. The fourth day the steering gear got out of order. The engines were stopped and the boat began to roll heavily. In a little while many became seasick and there was a rush for the rails. The machine was repaired by ten o'clock; it was our first and only case of trouble with the ship.

One afternoon an orthodox betrothal party was held on the fore deck. The affianced couple were both orthodox *khalutsim.* The groom-to-be, a serious looking fellow with spectacles, was twenty-two; his fiancée, Bella Gutfriend, was also twenty-two. She was all blushes and looked as though she would faint with pleasure when the traditional plate was broken at the end of the ceremony. I was an honored guest since I had been asked to use my influence to obtain a plate from the galley for the party. Both young people were Polish Jews who had met at a *hachshara.*

The bride's father, a short, bearded Jew, all smiles in his shirtsleeves, black mohair vest, gold watch chain, and *yarmilke,* was the only relative present. The ceremony was performed by the leader of this orthodox group, a fine looking man named Moses Lieberman from Carpatho-Russia who had fought as a Czech officer on the Russian front for two and a half years. He said his grandmother was an aunt of Adolf Zuckor, the film magnate.

After the ceremony everybody danced the *hora.* The dancing and singing went on for the rest of the afternoon. One of the songs was a Hebrew song set to the tune of "Onward Christian Soldiers."

At 4:30 o'clock the afternoon of the sixth day out all passengers were summoned to a meeting on the foredeck. They were addressed from the bridge by a *Haganah* worker. He gave them instructions about how they should act if they were captured and questioned by the British. There were cheers and applause when he said:

"As far as we are concerned, you are already citizens of *Eretz Israel,* whatever the English say."

He warned that there were still many difficulties ahead, but one of his warnings created a reaction that seemed natural to all of us.

"For a while you may find that you have not gone to *Eretz,* but to a prison in *Eretz.*"

There was a burst of relieved laughter. Prison didn't matter so long as it was a prison in *Eretz.*

"There you'll see barbed wire again," he continued.

There were chuckles of satisfaction from the crowd. Barbed wire didn't matter either.

The meeting and the instructions caused a stir. Everybody felt that the end of our journey must be near.

We were told to line up on deck and proceed one by one to the captain's cabin, where we would be given our illegal immigration certificates.

We each filled out a blue certificate printed in Hebrew on one side and in English on the other. It was called, "Permit To Enter Palestine." We wrote in our name, the names of our parents, the place and date of our birth, and our nationality by birth. The certificate stated that we "had been found qualified by the representatives of the Jewish Community of Palestine for repatriation to *Eretz Israel.*"

The certificate cited four authorities for the Jewish community's action.

The first was from Ezekiel: "And they shall abide in the lands that I have given unto Jacob my servant, wherein your fathers abode, and they shall abide therein, even they, and their children, and their children's children, forever."

The second was from Isaiah: "With great mercies will I gather thee."

The third was *Lord Balfour's Declaration of 2 November 1917,* and the last was *The Mandate for Palestine.*

The underground worker, who had a sense of humor, signed the name "Reb Moishe Ben Maimon" in the space for the signature of the quarantine officer. Moses ben Maimon, known also by his Latin name of Maimonides, was a famous Hebrew philosopher and physician of the Middle Ages.

The next afternoon we sighted smoke rising as if from another ship behind a little island far to the east. Everybody was sent below. When we came up again we saw that the ship had steamed from behind the island and was on the horizon ahead of us. We heard that it was a Turkish ship. Ours seemed to be following it. We did not know then that this was to be our first and last Sabbath eve on the ship, or that this other boat was to play an eventful part in our lives.

In the captain's cabin, the evening Sabbath candles burned and orthodox women blessed the candles with the traditional prayers. After dinner the foredeck was given over to the orthodox Jews for Sabbath services. A few in the crew joined them. The rest of us stood on the bridge watching. It was a moving scene.

We were headed due east. The light of the setting sun fell on the gray, blue, and gold of the prayer shawls as the pious among our passengers prayed and chanted, bowing over and over again to the east, where lay the Promised Land.

The next morning the Sabbath sky was blue and cloudless. Services were held on deck again, and as a special honor the captain and the underground *Haganah* emissary were called up to read the *Torah*. The captain was called up as the hero and he read the *Maftir,* the regular weekly portion from the prophets. The *Maftir* that morning had special significance for all of us. It was 66 Isiah 13, and those who understood Hebrew wept as they heard the words of the ancient prophecy:

"As one whom his mother comforteth, so will I comfort ye; and ye shall be comforted in Jerusalem."

IX

We were all ordered to pack our bags and have them ready the first thing in the morning. The order sent a thrill of excitement through the ship. That night everybody seemed to be singing. We all assumed that the sudden instructions meant that we would land in Palestine the next day.

On the foredeck the *khalutsim* danced a tremendous *hora.* They joined hands and swung around the deck, stamping out the beat and leaping with joy until it seemed that they would crash through the deck. I could bear to watch no longer and broke into the circle between two of my friends and danced with them. We danced until we were exhausted.

On the pretext that it was the birthday of a sweet-faced German-Jewish girl named Frieda, who was the hardest working of all the volunteers in the galley, the crew were invited to a surprise party in the mess. We all sang "Happy

Birthday," but we soon learned that the birthday was a subterfuge and that this was really a farewell to the ship.

Cake and coffee were served. The people sang Hebrew songs. I don't understand Hebrew and kept begging all evening that they sing some of the Yiddish songs I had heard on the way to Bratislava. Finally one of the *shomrim* explained:

"Those songs are too sad and bitter. They are the songs of the exile. Don't ask us to sing them. These Hebrew songs are the songs of our new life."

The Palestinian emissary sang a love song in Arabic which he had learned from Arab neighbors. They listened entranced. This, too, was Palestine for them.

When I went on deck the next morning I saw the other boat a few hundred yards away from us. It was a wooden freighter flying the Turkish flag. The name *Akbel II* and its home port, Istanbul, were painted on its stern. The refugees saw it with surprise. Soon word spread that we were to transfer to this other ship for the final leg of our journey.

The *Akbel,* a 250-ton freighter about half the length of our boat, was to tie up to us for the transfer. She maneuvered like a nervous old woman. Her captain ran excitedly up and down her bridge. His little mustache and his jerky movements made him look like Charlie Chaplin in an old-fashioned movie short. He had a whistle in his mouth and kept blowing on it and waving his arms for no apparent reason. His empty ship rode high in the water and rolled badly. Her deck would be now higher, now lower than ours.

While our passengers threw their luggage on our fore-deck the two ships moved back and forth, trying to get into position to tie up. At one time we touched, at another we actually caught ropes thrown from the fore and aft of the other ship. But each time we had to move away again. Once we bumped with a crash that damaged the port side of the Turkish boat. Her captain began shouting.

Our captain ran up on the bridge with a megaphone and yelled:

"Do you speak English?"

"Yes, I speak English," the other answered, but attempts at further conversation disclosed that this was about the limit of his English vocabulary.

The big Greek who was a pastry maker was summoned to the bridge and given the megaphone.

"Parlez Grec?" he shouted.

A man who seemed to be the first mate of the other boat shouted back:

"Oui! Oui!"

A conversation in Greek followed, with their first mate translating to the Turkish captain. On our bridge a Belgian translated the Greek Jew's French for our captain.

We learned that the Turkish captain was unwilling to risk tying up for fear our steel hull might stove in the side of his ship. He complained that his port side forward had already been damaged. It also became apparent that the Turkish captain was ready to call the whole deal off. He didn't seem anxious to take us on board.

The Turkish captain suddenly blew three blasts on his whistle, as though in farewell.

Nine of our huskiest men, including several ex-Partisans, climbed down the ladder into the motor launch we had lowered. One of them had a Jewish flag which he folded under his jacket. The others had pockets which bulged interestingly. We saw them reach the other ship and clamber up on its deck. Two men ran aft, one forward. The other six went on the bridge, and in a moment the Turkish captain and his first mate were surrounded.

What happened after that must have been pretty persuasive because from then on one of our men seemed to be in command. We could see another refugee arguing forcibly with two seamen on the deck of the other ship. They finally lowered one of the two lifeboats from the Turkish ship and began rowing toward us.

Both were barefoot and thin. One wore a ragged beret, the other looked as though his hair hadn't been combed since the Young Turk revolution. The one with the beret must have been a stoker. His face was as soot black as if he were made up for a minstrel show. Bright, intelligent, and friendly eyes twinkled out of the black face.

Blackface reached up a long oar which one of our sailors caught. The first of our men passengers began to climb down our ladder and into the boat. The transfer had begun.

The men were to go first, the women to follow later, with the sick and the doctor last of all. The women and the sick were lying all over the foredeck and the luggage. Some of them were very weak that morning and more than a little frightened at the prospect of that transfer on the open sea. The men waited aft and below deck, lining up in turn at the head of the ladder. On the other side, amidship, the doctor sat by the rail superintending his little corps of *Red Mogen Dovid* [Jewish Red Cross] workers, who kept running back and forth to help the sick. The doctor looked pretty sick himself.

Neither the crew nor the passengers had had breakfast that morning. One of the latter asked me if I could please get something for his wife who was feeling faint. I went down to the galley. Below deck everything was in confusion and the odor was terrific. Several people had fainted and were stretched out near the gangway.

I found hot coffee in a big restaurant type percolator. I poured myself a cup. It tasted good. I poured a pitcherful of the hot coffee, took some of the cups and put a loaf of bread under one arm. One of the nurses helped me give out coffee to those who looked sick, and I tore off pieces of bread for those who were hungry.

The doctor was green around the gills and I went back and got a glass of coffee for him and a chocolate bar I found in one of the drawers in the galley. I mixed powdered milk with water and carried a pitcher full of milk to the sick women. One gray-haired woman who was seasick asked for a lemon, but I learned there were only five left and that these had to be saved for our trip on the other boat. Some of the women became alarmed when we put lifebelts on them for the transfer. The atmosphere was like that of a shipwreck.

There was a cry of "Man overboard!" and we saw a man swimming toward the other ship. Halfway there he was picked up by a lifeboat and brought back. He was a young

Belgian who angrily claimed that he had permission to
swim to the other ship.

The women began to climb down the ladder. Their
courage was amazing. Some of them had to jump into the
arms of the sailors. One of our American crew members,
an ex-soldier, said:

"What it took amphibious troops weeks to learn, these
folks are doing without griping right off."

An elderly Jewish woman made a similar comment,
with great satisfaction:

"It looks as though Jews can still do things."

When I went up on the bridge to say good-by to the
crew I heard that the baggage was not to be transferred.
The transfer was taking longer than was counted on and
it was feared we might be caught by a British patrol boat.
We were only about a hundred miles from Palestine.

I protested that our people should have been told this
the night before. I said it didn't matter about their clothes,
but that many refugees had put photographs and other
precious mementoes of their vanished families in their
baggage. I knew how much these faded photographs of
wives, mothers, and children meant to them. In most cases
it was all they had left of their old lives. I was told that
the bags would have to be thrown overboard since that
mountain of luggage was bound to raise suspicion if seen
by a British patrol boat or plane. I begged the crew to at
least take out photographs and letters before throwing the
bags over.

"You'll have time this afternoon, after we leave," I
pleaded. "It would be like a second death for these people

to throw such mementoes away. Almost all these bags have names on them, but if you haven't time just dump all such personal things into one big bag and send them later to Palestine where these people can come and claim them."

They promised to do what they could.

I went off with the doctor and a boatload of sick women at 11:35. One woman cried in fright as we sped across the water. The last of the *shomrim* followed us to the Turkish boat and after that the crew brought huge crates with our lunches and some water. This took several trips.

I thought the transfer was completed when the motor launch arrived with a surprise—the boys were bringing our bags. It took an hour and half a dozen trips in the launch to transfer the baggage, and the crew members sweated like stevedores in the hot sun as they threw the bags on our deck.

Our passengers looked relieved to see their baggage. But it looked as though this transfer of baggage would prove disastrous. For just as the launch arrived with the last of the bags a warship came over the horizon to the north of us.

There was a cry from the launch:

"Let's get the hell outa here."

We all waved and cheered, but we watched anxiously as the launch sped across the four hundred yards or more that separated our two ships.

The warship, looming ever larger, bore down upon us. It looked as though all was lost.

X

I have never seen anything which seemed quite as large as that warship, its gray, menacing bulk growing ever larger, its huge guns pointed directly at us.

We could see the motor launch, in a final burst of speed, reach the ship on which we had sailed. We could see tiny figures clamber up the rope like monkeys on a vine. We watched others haul the launch on deck. And then the ship went off due west at a fast clip, like a swift hare running from a giant hound.

On our little Turkish cargo boat, a bell rang. The ancient engines turned and we started off in the opposite direction, due east. The worn timber creaked and the ship shook as her engines strained. Our maximum speed was about seven knots. It was like being in one of those nightmares in which one can barely move one's feet in flight from an advancing menace.

Since the two illegal vessels were going in opposite directions, our pursuer had to choose between us. We hoped the oncoming warship would set off after us. The boat we were on was a worthless old tub which had little chance of running the British blockade successfully anyway. The ship we had left was a swift and valuable vessel for which other refugees were already waiting in a south European port.

For a minute it looked as though the warship was head-

ing for our first boat. We raised the *Mogen Dovid* to the
top of our mast and then pulled it down again in the hope
that this disclosure of our identity as a Jewish refugee ship
would bring the warship in pursuit. It did, but not for the
reason we expected. As the great ship headed across our
bow, her decks crowded with sailors, we saw the flag of
another great nation flying from her mast aft. Our tense
refugees broke into a tremendous cheer. There was a great
waving of hats and shouting of greetings across the water.

The warship was a big supercruiser. The British have
begun to place protests with every nation which shows any
friendliness to Jewish refugees trying to get to Palestine,
and I do not want to create any difficulties for that naval
commander or his country. But I don't imagine he was
ever cheered so enthusiastically as he was that day by our
refugees.

The ship from which we had transferred reached the
western horizon and stopped as if to see what was happen-
ing to us. When the warship resumed her course our old
ship started up again and in a few minutes disappeared
over the horizon. The warship went south and also vanished over the horizon.

Our little freighter was alone on that vast and ancient
sea. She plowed along wearily, her engines wheezing like
an asthmatic old woman. Her hull was low in the water
from the weight of her unusual cargo. Her main deck and
her three small upper decks, fore, aft, and amidships, were
packed as tightly with people as a rush-hour subway. Sick
and exhausted women had even invaded the wheelhouse
and were lying all over its floor and on the back bench

and around the feet of the harassed Turkish pilot. The wheelhouse was the only cool spot on the ship.

Amidships there was an ancient salon with a galley in which our precious supply of water was stored and guarded. Off the entrance to the salon was a water closet, the only one on the ship. It stank heartily. The dingy, dark, and unfurnished salon beyond was filled with people. Even the grimy stokehold in which two profusely sweating and blackened stokers were at work was filled with refugees, their faces pale and drawn.

The worst places of all on the ship were the two cargo holds. In these holds, 'tween decks had been newly built to increase the amount of passenger space. The holds were open to the sky. The 'tween decks provided a kind of balcony around them, just high enough for refugees to sit in them. The only air and light came from the opening on deck. Inside, the holds were dark, dank, and fearfully hot, much more like a den for wild animals than a habitation for human beings. One narrow ladder led down into each hold. A guard stood on deck at the top of the ladder. His function became clearer as that hot and cloudless summer day wore on.

To move around the ship was a slow and painful job. One did not try it often. One had to climb over people sitting or lying on the deck. It was hard to avoid stepping on them. They lay exhausted and irritable from the fierce heat. All were hungry and thirsty.

It was after three before the guards could open the crates containing food and water. There was an emergency lunch packed in separate paper bags for each one of us.

The galley crew on the old ship must have stayed up all night preparing those lunches.

For the orthodox, the lunch bag contained a hardtack jelly sandwich made of two pieces of big round biscuit smeared with grape jelly. The biscuits were so hard they had to be broken on the rail. There was a handful of currants and a big bar of chocolate. The non-kosher packages also had a bar of chocolate, two pieces of hardtack and a big slice of bologna in place of the jelly. We tackled the lunches with famished zest. This was the only food we were to have for two days and nights.

While we were eating, the *shomrim* passed around with big cans of water, the kind of cans stowed away on lifeboats for use in case of shipwreck. We all got a few sips from the dirty glasses carried by the guards and passed from hand to hand. The water was warm and stale, but to us it tasted good.

I had squeezed into a place near the doctor and his wife on the upper deck amidships. We sat with our backs against the hatch which provided a little air for the hot noisome stokehold below. Every once in a while one of the stokers, his face black with soot, would climb up for a bit of air and sit grinning like a cheerful bogeyman at the girls. The stokers never opened their mouths throughout the voyage. I suppose they spoke only Turkish, but they might have been deaf mutes as far as we were concerned.

That Turkish freighter might have been a fine boat in the days of Abdul Hamid, but its engines now shook as if they would break down any minute. It was horribly over-

loaded and leaned crazily in the water whenever there
were more people on one side than the other.

We had to make a fateful decision. Should we try to
run the British blockade, or should we ask for help? The
Haganah emissary on board was afraid that some mishap might capsize or sink the ship with all aboard. The
British blockading forces by that time on the sea and in
the air were so numerous that even a faster ship could
hardly hope to land its cargo secretly in Palestine. He decided it would be best to send out an SOS and give ourselves up voluntarily to the British rather than risk a
disaster.

The SOS went out over the portable wireless we had
brought on board. Distress flags were raised. Shortly before five o'clock a two-engined plane zoomed out of the
east and flew so low over our boat that it created a welcome passing breeze. It circled and recircled around us.
A little later a four-engined plane repeated the same per-
formance. After dark, patrol planes dropped flares around
the boat. But after the first flares no planes returned and
we were left alone and apprehensive on that dark and
gloomy sea.

That night was the worst I had yet spent. I was to
learn that night, and to learn the hard and feverish way,
what life in a concentration camp had been like.

We had no more food and little water left. We feared
that at any moment the frightfully overloaded boat might
capsize or sink. Our SOS seemed to have been to no avail.
Though British planes had circled the afternoon and
dropped red flares around us shortly after sunset, there

was no further sign of help that night on the dark and lonely sea. We thought we were about one hundred miles from Palestine and we assumed that we were headed in that direction. We were to learn differently in the morning.

The most terrible problem of all that night was to get the men to take turns going down into the hold. There wasn't enough space on the decks of the ship to accommodate all of us. We had to take turns. The holds were packed with men. Our *shomrim* were supposed to see that those in the hold were allowed to come up on deck every few hours and men on deck required to take their places below. A bitter battle went on constantly—not many men were willing to give up a place in the open air to go down into the unlighted, hot, and stinking hold.

A few went below voluntarily. Some went shamefaced after the guards had explained and pleaded. But some sat silent and stubborn while the *shomrim* cried hoarsely, furiously, and impotently for men to go below. I heard one cry in Yiddish, *"Khaveyrim, ikh red tsu mentshen, nit beheymes"* [Comrades, I am talking to men, not beasts]. Another pleaded, *"Ikh hob nit keyn revolver, ikh red tsu aykh als mentshen"* [I don't have a revolver, I'm pleading with you as men]. But with many, all pleas were unavailing. Some had to be picked up bodily and carried to the hold. Fist fights broke out.

I was on the upper deck. A *shomer* came up the ladder looking for men who were not too ill to be sent below. He yanked a big blond German-looking fellow to his feet. But the latter, his face livid, shouted:

"I was in that hold all day long when others were on deck. I can't stand it any more. I swear by my mother that if you try to take me down there I'll strangle you with my own hands."

He raised his hands as if to grab the *shomer's* throat. He looked mad enough to do so. The *shomer* backed down.

The scene from the upper deck might have been something out of the *Inferno.* The deck was dimly lit. In the center of the deck was the entrance to the hold. It sounded as though a riot were in progress below. Big fat Rudy, the ex-circus strong man, who was leader of the *shomrim,* fought his way about on deck, naked to the waist. He had a whistle in his mouth and alternately blew sharp blasts and issued hoarse shouts of command as he superintended the transfer of men from the deck to the hold. The engines beat regularly and interminably like the tom-toms of a heathen god to whom we were all waiting to be sacrificed, and the mass of struggling men below seemed to be a kind of weird and hellish ballet.

I was a privileged character, allowed the run of the ship and a place on the upper deck. I had climbed to a seat on the boom where I could hold on to the mast and get a good view of the ship and the sea. But I felt like a slacker and so climbed down on the lower deck and pushed my way through the quarreling men to the guards at the opening of the hold.

"It's the journalist," somebody yelled.

"He doesn't have to go down there," Rudy shouted hoarsely.

But I said I wanted to take my turn with the rest and Rudy let me climb down the ladder into the hold.

At the foot of the ladder men were fighting for a chance to climb up. I forced my way through the tight-packed crowd to a place where I could sit against the far wall. When one got used to it, the darkness was not complete. A faint red glow came through the opening. It was frightfully hot. I fought and pushed for room in which to strip to the waist. The air was sickening, the noise almost unbearable; the sensible thing was to sit and sweat and keep quiet.

The people around me were hot and angry and irritable and not at all friendly. In that dark and noisy dungeon nobody had the strength to think of anything but himself. There was a constant milling about as new people arrived from the deck and others already below tried to fight their way back to the foot of the ladder. A newcomer pushed his way over to me and yelled with a curse that I was sitting on his bag and that I had his place. He was beside himself with rage over being sent back into the hold. He scared me. I got up and pushed my way through to another part of the hold where I squeezed in along the wall among other snarling, irritable shipmates.

The heat, noise, and bad air drained away the strength of all but the strongest and fiercest. These gradually pushed and fought their way to the center under the opening while the weaker were left sitting or standing in the darker, almost airless, sections under the 'tween decks. Those at the foot of the ladder fought among themselves to stay there and tried to climb up. The guard kept pushing them down; there was a violent interchange of blows and curses.

A few of the cleverer, stronger, and more unscrupulous seemed to get back on deck after less than ten minutes below. But some had been in that hold for hours, and a few in the darkest far corners may well have been there since they came on board. They seemed too utterly spent to move. A kind of fierce Darwinian struggle went on in that hold and in that struggle the men seemed to become less than human. It was like being in a den of wolves.

I spent almost two hours in the hold and then began to struggle and push forward to get my hands and feet on that coveted ladder. I had had enough. To breathe the fresh air and to see the stars again even from that incredibly crowded and dirty deck was a relief no words can adequately describe. It was as though one had emerged from a prison or a concentration camp. I imagined that this was how men fought and snarled in a *KZ*. I later asked friends on board and they told me that the spirit and atmosphere of the hold was that of concentration camps in which they had been. The *KZ* bred a subhuman individualism. Everyone had to fight for sleeping space, for bread, for a breath of air, for life itself.

On deck I ran into a German psychologist friend who had also been in the hold. I had never seen a man's face so changed in a few hours. He looked exhausted. His face was drawn, one eye was strained and out of focus. The pleasant young man I knew had the look of a creature cowering under oppression. He must have looked that way when he was in Buchenwald.

I confess with shame that I never again volunteered to go down into the hold. It was more than I could take. I felt shaky when I came up on deck and begged one of the *shomrim* to haul up a bucket of sea water and throw it over me as I leaned far over the rail. The shock of the cold water was delicious and refreshing and I begged for another shower. Afterwards I went up on the upper deck. The doctor and his wife made room for me under the boom. I slept there sitting up.

I got up around four and climbed up on the boom. The sky was growing light. At 4:35 the red sun rose out of the sea to disclose two surprises. There were high mountains on our left which I thought must be the mountains of Lebanon, but they turned out to be those of Cyprus. Our Turkish captain, perhaps losing his nerve, had been taking us away from Palestine.

The second surprise, about a mile away on our starboard side, was a British destroyer. It was waiting to close in on us like a greyhound of the sea.

XI

We were about eighty miles farther from our goal than we had been at the point of transfer.

We didn't know what the attitude of the British would be. We hoped that the destroyer had come in answer to our SOS, that they would take a few of our sick on board

their ship, perhaps give us some food and water and tow
us into Haifa. Perhaps we had too high an opinion of
British gallantry.

The British moved closer and we read that the number
of this destroyer was R-75 and its name the *Virago*. When
it came alongside one of the *shomrim* handed me a megaphone and asked me to talk to the British.

"Hullo, hullo! We're in a bad way. Can you give us a
tow to Haifa?" I shouted across the water.

Sailors on the deck of the destroyer pulled the covers
off a lifeboat and lowered it into the sea. Six sailors and
an ensign got into the boat and began to row toward our
ship. Aboard they made their way gingerly to the wheel
house. Many people lay underfoot, too sick or exhausted
to move. The British sailors stepped over them carefully.
They wore white shorts. Their officer, a fledgling ensign,
tried hard to look imperturbable.

"Who's spokesman for these people?" the officer asked
me.

"Ikh ken nit reden English [I can't speak English],"
I answered in Yiddish.

I was taking no chances on being taken off that boat
by the British before I could reach Palestine. I waved my
hand to my German friend. He spoke a rather awkward
English with a strong Dutch accent. He had learned
English in Holland before the war.

I have never seen a more complicated bit of linguistics
than the interrogation of our Turkish captain by the British ensign. The ensign spoke English with that calm assur-
ance Englishmen seem to have abroad that they will of

course be understood. It took a chain of translators, however, to make this possible.

The ensign spoke to my German friend in English. The
German translated this into Hebrew. One of our Greeks
stood by and interpreted the Hebrew into broken Russian
for one of the Turkish sailors, who, in turn, translated for
the Turkish captain.

One of the British sailors stood at the top of the wheel
house with two signal flags. In his white shorts, bare knees
and brown, heavy socks he looked like an enlarged Boy
Scout. His name, satisfyingly enough, turned out to be
Popham.

Another sailor with a message pad stood beside the
ensign. They were surrounded by an unwashed horde of
refugees, your correspondent included.

The ensign, flustered by the stares of the women, some
of whom didn't look too unattractive even on that dreadful
morning, handed a knife to the sailor with which to
sharpen a stub of a pencil. He proceeded to dictate the
results of his interrogation.

The sailor wrote it all down respectfully, rereading it
aloud for the benefit of Popham, who signaled it across
the water to the destroyer. The ensign dictated, much like
a businessman in an office, pausing nervously over his
choice of words. At one point his youthful upper class
dignity broke down completely and he shouted to the
sailor on the wheelhouse:

"Did you get that, Pop?"

But otherwise he addressed him as "Pop'm."

The most important question asked by the ensign was

whether we were willing voluntarily to be towed into
Haifa. There was a good reason for this question. We were
outside Palestinian territorial waters. Under international
law the British have no right to seize a boat on the high
seas, even if they know for a certainty that it is carrying
unauthorized immigrants to Palestine. On two occasions
the British have been ordered by their own courts in Palestine to return Jewish ships captured on the high seas. On
the other hand, if an illegal boat voluntarily submits to
British jurisdiction on the high seas the seizure is of course
a legal one.

We told the ensign that we were willing to submit to
British authority and asked him to tow us into Haifa.

The ensign dictated to the destroyer, "Severe engine
trouble, plus overcrowding, made it impossible to proceed,"
and that we would place ourselves voluntarily under
British authority to be towed in. A big signal lamp on the
destroyer twinkled back a question:

"Is there enough food and water on board?"

The ensign answered that we were out of both, and
stood nervously twiddling his pencil against his pants
under the stares of the numb and savage horde surrounding him. He was thin, blond, of somewhat more than
medium height. He looked the picture of a well-bred
English boy of good family. He was obviously distressed
by our plight. My friends and I liked him.

The ensign asked whether we had a towline aboard.
We hadn't. Then he asked if we could clear the foredeck
so that a towline could be attached to our boat. *Shomrim*

made their way slowly and painfully to the foredeck to clear a path, but with little success.

The foredeck was packed tight with girls and women. They had slept leaning against each other. The lucky ones had sat all night at the railing, their feet hanging over the water. They were dazed, sleepy, tired, and resentful. Each was afraid to move lest she lose her precious space.

I megaphoned an appeal to them in my rather inadequate Yiddish.

"Comrades," I pleaded, "the British officer on board is a kind man and he is offering to tow us into Haifa. That means we can be in *Eretz* this evening. You must clear the foredeck so that a towline can be attached to the British destroyer. Please move and make place so that when the British sailors come back on board they will have room."

A few began to move off the upper deck and down the rail. Some of those on the deck below should have moved into the cargo hold and made room for the women from the upper deck, and some did. But the hold itself was jammed with men clamoring for a chance to get up into the light and air.

In the meantime the ensign and his six sailors climbed back into the lifeboat in which they had come and started back to the destroyer. We watched them hopefully. We were hungry and thirsty and hoped for food and water.

The *shomrim* were busy on both decks, forcing men into the hold and bringing women down from the foredeck. It looked as though the English would save us after all.

We were in for an unpleasant surprise. We saw the ensign and the six sailors go aboard the destroyer. Then we saw tiny figures hoisting the lifeboat on board. We wondered why, since a boat would be needed to bring us food and water.

The destroyer began to move and for one relieved moment we thought it was maneuvering into position to attach a towline to our cargo boat. But the distance between us widened. The destroyer sailed off to the east.

This destruction of our hopes was so unexpected that our reaction was one of dulled amazement rather than indignation. No one shouted or cursed or shook a fist at the vanishing British destroyer. We just watched it in silence. The destroyer grew smaller and smaller and finally vanished over the horizon.

"It will be a miracle if we ever get to *Eretz,*" the doctor said.

XII

The second day and night on the Turkish cargo boat were the worst I ever spent. The British destroyer steamed off shortly after 7 A.M. without giving us food and water or the tow into Haifa for which we had asked. We were to the south of Cyprus, about 180 miles from Palestine. The sky was cloudless and the sea calm but the day was brutally hot.

The boat from which we had transferred on the seas early the previous morning had given us water and provisions for but one day. Had our Turkish captain sailed straight for Palestine we would have reached there that night. Either he had lost his way or his nerve and headed north instead of east. We were eighty miles further away from Palestine than we had been at our transfer point.

Some people on board still had the remains of the lunch bag given us the day before but there was very little water; all we had were a few precious and closely guarded regulation cans of water, the kind packed on lifeboats in case of shipwreck, and it was over water that our first crisis that day was to arise.

The heat was sickening. There were a score or more of people on board, including four pregnant women and a cardiac case who had to be given injections at regular intervals. The doctor was on the upper deck amidships with a small store of medicines. He was ill himself, and our *Red Mogen Dovid* workers would come to him during the day for medicines and instructions.

On the lower deck one of the *shomrim* had attached a rope to a bucket and given showers to those who wanted them. The men would strip to the waist and lean far over the side. A *shomrim* would pull up a bucket of water and throw it over them. I had one every hour or so during the day. The shock of the cold water was very refreshing.

I got another bucket and tied a rope to it and had one of the *shomrim* fill it and hand it up to the top deck amidships, where there were many men and women sick with the heat and thirst. I went around with the bucket sprinkling water over the needy and wetting handkerchiefs so people could put them on their foreheads. The women didn't like the shock of the water; the men did, even one sick old man I called *zeyde* [grandpa] but who told me he had neither children nor grandchildren.

The men stretched blankets as awnings against the sun. People lay down under the lifeboats where there was a bit of shade and even around the hot smokestack. Most of them were too miserable to think of anyone but themselves.

Tempers wore very thin on the boat. It was difficult to keep a way open to the wheelhouse and to make people take turns in the hot hold. One *shomer* said to me in exasperation, *"Yiden un ferd zaynen di zelbe zakh— beyde miz men trayben"* [Jews and horses are the same thing—you have to drive both of them]. I'm afraid I lost my temper several times and I apologize to those of my comrades whose feelings I may have hurt.

At one point I was trying to make room on the starboard side amidships for a sick woman. A boy of about twelve was sitting there. I asked him to give up his place. He refused, and a woman near him whom I took to be his mother looked indignantly at me. I yanked him to his feet, shouting:

"What do you mean you won't give your place to a sick woman. If you don't want to be a *mentsh* [man] don't go to *Eretz.*"

The word *mentsh* is richer in Yiddish than in English and has a richer connotation of manliness.

The boy moved away resentfully, but later I saw him

helping to put up a blanket as an awning and shouting to another boy:

"Come on, help! If you want to go to *Eretz* you must be a *mentsh*."

"Now you're acting like a real *khaluts*," I said, patting him on the back.

In my water-soaked notebook for that day there is this notation:

"I feel sick. No water yet today. I found a piece of hardtack under the boom. Someone else had eaten part of it. I chewed on the rest with relish. I had an odd experience I have read about in stories of shipwreck. The hardtack did not dissolve or even grow wet in my mouth. I had no saliva. It pulverized, and I swallowed it dry."

The one cool spot on the boat was the wheelhouse. I had a nap there in the afternoon, and found an opened tin of concentrated lifeboat rations. I ate a biscuit and a chocolate tablet and had a tiny mouthful of brackish water from a very dirty glass. I rinsed my mouth with the water before swallowing. It might have been nectar, it tasted so delicious.

Four sick women were lying on the floor around the wheelhouse.

The shortage of water precipitated a crisis in the afternoon. There was a terrific fight on the lower deck and a lot of shouting. Rudy jumped on the stairs leading to the afterdeck and yelled:

"I take over all power on this boat and order the *shomrim* to distribute the rest of the water."

He was finally calmed down, but not until he was

promised that one of our last remaining cans of water would be passed around.

I felt guilty that evening because of a special treat. I was near the wheelhouse and looked in to see the Turkish captain in his pajamas eating his dinner and drinking tea. The crew had a small store of food and a spirit lamp with which they prepared tea. I looked at the tea so longingly that he invited me to have a cup. It was hot and sweet and I have never tasted anything quite so good. I insisted on giving him one of my last packs of Camels in return.

That night there was a panic. The barometer began to fall. There was a dead calm on the sea, as if before a storm. About eleven o'clock the captain became alarmed. He was afraid the boat would capsize in a storm. His fear spread to the *shomrim* who began to herd people off the decks and into the holds. Fights broke out and women became hysterical. Word spread that a storm was coming and that the boat might sink. Even some of the best of the women *khalutsim* lost their nerve.

We sent out an SOS. About two in the morning a British destroyer came alongside. It turned floodlights on us and we saw the number R-75 on its sides, the same number as the boat which had refused us aid the previous morning.

I handled the megaphone:

"Is that the *Virago?*"

I repeated the question, but again got no answer.

We asked how far we were from Haifa.

"Thirty-five miles," was the reply.

"The barometer's falling," I shouted, "and our captain

is afraid that we may go under in a storm. We're terribly overloaded. Could you take some of our sick people on board and give us a tow to Haifa?"

We waited but got no answer.

"Won't you please answer?" I asked. There was no answer.

I tried again.

"Won't you please answer?"

There was no reply this time either.

The captain had shut off our engines and the whole ship waited anxiously for some response.

"Won't you please answer?" I asked for the third time.

But they remained silent.

One of the *shomrim* standing near me said:

"The hell with the bastards."

We waited about fifteen minutes. I picked up the megaphone and shouted derisively:

"Thank you."

We started up our engines to a full six or seven knots and started off for Haifa.

In spite of our fears and a rough sea, we avoided a storm. Shortly before dawn I slept for a while on top of the wheelhouse. I woke to see the dim outlines of a mountain toward the southeast.

As the light increased and the sun rose, a cry ran over the ship.

"It's *Eretz Israel.*"

We saw Mount Carmel ahead of us, and the town of Haifa sleeping in the morning sun below us. In the harbor as we came in we saw what seemed to be a whole British fleet waiting for us.

The refugees cheered and began to sing *"Hatikvah,"* the Jewish national anthem. We pulled down the Turkish flag at our helm and raised the *Mogen Dovid* and the Union Jack side by side. People jumped for joy, kissed and hugged each other on the deck.

So singing we moved into the arms of the waiting British, in *Eretz* at last.

XIII

I must give the British credit for a bit of gallantry on our entrance into Haifa harbor. The same destroyer, R-75, the HMS *Virago*, which had twice refused us aid, was the warship assigned to take us over in the harbor. A small boat with six men and an officer, but not the same young ensign who had been on board before, came out from the *Virago* and was followed by another boatload of Palestinian Arab police.

The officer, with the Palestinian Arabs in their lambskin hats clearing a way for him, first went to the wheelhouse and said: "I take possession of this ship." Then he ordered a sailor to change the flag at our foremast. There on entering the harbor we had pulled down the Turkish flag and raised the *Mogen Dovid* — the blue-and-white Jewish flag—side by side with the Union Jack.

Much to our surprise the British did not pull down the Jewish flag but only the Union Jack. The Union Jack we had raised was the merchant marine Union Jack, the Union Jack on a field of red. That was the proper flag for us as a merchant vessel, albeit illegal. In taking possession the British replaced our Union Jack with the Royal Ensign and allowed us to proceed into Haifa with our Jewish flag flying.

So we moved closer to frizzly Mount Carmel, with stucco-colored Haifa on its northern flank. Watching our arrival were a half dozen warships in the harbor, and, far away along the docks, crowds of people. We felt proud and exultant to arrive with the Jewish flag at our mast.

The refugees looked for the first time upon the Holy Land with wondering and often tear-filled eyes. This was the sight for which they had longed with all their hearts, the sight for which they had risked their lives crossing one illegal border after another and on the high seas.

I was standing near the wheelhouse. The British officer stood beside me.

"I thought it was very sporting of us this morning to send up the Union Jack as well as the *Mogen Dovid*," I said. "But I must say I think you fellows were very sporting, too, to leave our *Mogen Dovid* up there when you raised your Royal Ensign."

The officer, a young and pleasant chap, smiled and said:

"Well, we English are a sporting people."

Then, noticing my accent, he asked curiously:

"Have you ever been to America?"

He didn't ask whether I was an American. It must have

seemed too fantastic to him to expect an American to be on that boat. By that time, dirty and unshaven, I looked like the other DP's on board. I had no intention of being taken off until I was ready to go, so I only answered:

"Yes, I've been to America."

The British officer then broke some amazing news.

"You probably haven't heard," he said, "that there have been widespread raids in Palestine on the Jewish Agency and the leadership of the *Haganah*. Athlit, the detention camp to which refugees are usually taken, is full of Jewish leaders and you people will be held in the harbor."

When I heard this I decided to show my papers and try to get off the ship as soon as possible.

"In that case," I said, "I might as well show you my passport. I'm an American newspaperman and I had intended going along to Athlit so I could write about conditions inside the camp. But since we're to be held in the harbor I guess my mission's done and I might as well start for home."

I pulled out my green American passport and showed the British visa for Palestine which I had obtained at the British Embassy in Washington. The officer looked at them and then at me.

"Why the devil did you ever come on a tub like this?" he asked. "You must be the only legal passenger on board."

I said I was and explained that I came as a newspaperman in order to be able at write at first hand of the Jewish immigration to Palestine.

"Now that you know what conditions are like," the officer asked, "would you do it again?"

"Sure," I answered. "I had a wonderful time."

Some of my comrades stood listening curiously to this conversation. Then one of the girls voiced the only real fear that my fellow passengers felt. She said to me in Yiddish:

"Do you think the British might send us back?"

I translated the question for the officer and he smiled and said:

"No, we wouldn't do that. We British aren't that bad."

After I translated the answer to my relieved comrades the officer began to explain the British side of the matter.

"You people must realize," he said, "that the British are good friends of the Jews, but we have many other problems in our Empire and can't do everything we'd like to do."

This was before the British began forcibly removing illegal immigrants to Cyprus.

A police cutter came alongside and an officer asked in Hebrew how many sick we had aboard. The doctor told him there were about twenty-four and asked for help. A half hour later the cutter returned with a Palestinian-Jewish doctor and they began to remove the sick.

Water was brought aboard at ten o'clock. We passed down canteens to be filled for our sick, but no one paid too much attention to us. It was noon before we all had enough water.

Our boat had been renamed the *Beria,* in honor of the famous settlement the Jews had built up in Palestine that spring, in defiance of the British who had once razed it to the ground. The ship was taken into an inner part of the harbor, away from the town, and moored inside an artificial breakwater which was surrounded by a high iron fence. Eight illegal ships, including the *Sir Josiah,* were lined up there. We were transferred to the *Max Nordau,* which had brought a thousand immigrants from Rumania the month before.

An unpleasant surprise awaited us. On board the *Nordau* we were told that two cases of suspected bubonic plague had been found among the sick taken off the *Beria* and that we would be quarantined in the harbor for ten days or two weeks.

The *Max Nordau* was a change for the better. It was larger than the *Beria* and the decks were swept and clean.

Our people began to promenade the decks, chatting happily among themselves and gazing curiously at the land they had so hoped to see.

The Jewish community of Haifa sent food aboard: fresh white rolls, red tomatoes, and green peppers, white cream cheese, individual pint bottles of *laban,* the thick sour milk of the Levant, and big bunches of grapes.

Each of us was given a pint of *laban,* a big bunch of grapes, two rolls, a generous helping of the cheese, two tomatoes, and a pepper. The grapes were not quite in season and were very expensive. Their sweet juice and the cool *laban* were blissful food for parched throats after our long thirst. It must have cost a fortune to provide that lunch for us. It is no small matter to feed a thousand people and we were but one of the many thousands who had been arriving at that port since the war had ended. We ate heartily and gratefully.

But we were soon to find out that in some ways we had made a change for the worse. The *Max Nordau* was fitted out below deck with the same kind of temporary wooden bunks, four or five deep, on which we had slept on our first boat. The difference was that since the ship was lying idle in the harbor, with no steam up, there was no power to flush the bilges, to work the ventilators, or to provide current for the lights.

I got a rough wooden bunk with no mattress and several gaps in the wood. But I was one of the lucky ones, for my bunk was in an ancient stateroom on deck. It had a window and I shared it with only one person, a young *Red Mogen Dovid* worker, a Dutch boy named Perite. We had a washroom with a washstand but no water, and a small table. We felt among the privileged of the earth and invited our friends to take turns sleeping in the cabin during the day.

But the others were not so fortunate: to sleep below decks was sheer torture. There was a terrible odor from the unflushed latrines which pervaded the sleeping quarters. It was fearfully hot. At night there was a constant symphony of moans, sighs, whispered conversations. Few could sleep, and the refugees came on deck early in the morning looking haggard, bleary eyed, and at the end of their resources.

There was very little water and everyone felt the need of a wash. We begged for pint bottles of water from the galley or stood in long lines to fill our canteens at the slow-running tap below decks. The men had to shave out of pint bottles or canteens. The women tried their best to

wash up a bit, and to comb their hair, but it was difficult
to do after ten days without a bath.

So long as we had been on the way to *Eretz* the goal
was enough to keep people's spirits up. But once we
arrived, tantalizingly within sight of *Eretz,* yet not there,
to be prisoners in what the refugees regarded as their
homeland, to live in stink, filth and wretchedness, was
more than the best of the *khalutsim* could bear.

The assistant chief superintendent of the harbor, a
British official, came on board and asked to see the American journalist. I showed him my passport and visa and he
made a note of their numbers and said he was satisfied
that I was a legal immigrant. But when I asked when I
could leave, he said that was up to the medical authorities
since the ship was in quarantine.

When a Palestinian-Jewish health officer came aboard
later, he told me that I would have to stay on board with
the others until the quarantine was lifted, which would
be not less than ten days. I was lined up with the rest and
given a shot in the arm for bubonic plague by a British
doctor, who did a very skillful job, and treated us well.

I was determined to get off that boat. I did a little
investigating of my own. Our refugee doctor told me that
while the British were justified in taking all precautions,
the two suspected cases of bubonic plague were not that
at all but cases of swollen glands. He said the tests at the
hospital in Haifa, as reported to him that morning by the
health authorities, confirmed his diagnosis. He also said
that with Athlit and other detention camps full of arrested
Jewish leaders, the British would probably use quarantine

as an excuse to keep us on the boat. I decided I was going.

The day before I had sat on deck too tired and beaten to move. I felt that if anyone tried to talk to me I'd burst into tears. But after a night's sleep, even on that wooden bunk, I felt chipper again. I got a bottle of water and shaved, and then another bottle and took a sponge bath. I found out that at seven in the evening a cutter would take the doctor and some others ashore. I would take a chance.

I put on my U. S. military correspondent's uniform in the afternoon, packed my bags and said good-by to my friends. Just before seven o'clock, when the cutter came alongside, I walked down the gangplank with my bags and got on the cutter.

Perhaps it was the uniform. Perhaps it was my manner, which took for granted that I was leaving. The doctor probably thought I had the permission of the military, and the military assumed that I had the permission of the doctor. Anyway, no one asked me any questions.

I'll never forget the farewell I got as the cutter moved away from the boat. Word had spread that I was going to try to get away and everybody was on deck to see me off. It had meant something to everybody's morale to have an American newspaper correspondent on board and I had made many friends. These Jews were my own people and I had come to love them on our long trip together.

They waved and cheered and cried *sholom*. I stood on the cutter among the rather startled Britishers on board and shouted *sholom* and threw kisses to my friends and comrades. They were fortunate, for they were among the last shiploads of illegal immigrants permitted to land. They were not sent to Cyprus. After a stay in Athlit detention camp, they were set free, and since returning home I have had happy letters from three of my friends of the voyage.

The cutter pulled away. The ship grew smaller and vanished. Haifa loomed up ahead of me. At the dock I walked off. The immigration offices were closed but I went through customs and out the gates. An Arab guard who knew the doctor who had come ashore with me gave us a friendly *sholom.*

My underground journey to Palestine had ended. I was in *Eretz* at last.

Epilogue

I

When I reached Cairo after leaving Palestine I had luncheon with a group of friends I had made on my previous trip to the Middle East. The conversation turned, of course, to Palestine and the Jewish problem. Some of my friends have the Arab point of view, some the British. Some favored one supposed solution, some another. I found myself curiously uninterested in all their talk.

I had begun to feel like a DP myself on my underground trip to Palestine, and I found myself reacting like a DP during that luncheon debate. In presenting these conclusions to my trip, I hope I may be pardoned if in

215

taking leave of a memorable journey and memorable comrades I speak first as one of them.

For my comrades, for the Jews waiting in the DP camps of Germany and Austria, for the Jews fleeing across the borders of Eastern and Central Europe from new persecution, there is no longer a problem. Palestine is not a matter of theory.

Have they any choice? Is any country opening its doors to them? Has anything come of the endless conferences on refugees—the months of talk before the war, when many of the dead 6,000,000 might still have been saved; the endless negotiations and investigations since, when there are so few left?

Not all my comrades were heroes or idealists. Many of them would prefer life in a settled country like America or England to the hardships and struggle of the frontier in *Eretz*. But for most of them, Palestine is not merely the one possibility for a new life, is not merely a place of refuge, but *the country to which they want to go.* I met people in the DP camps and I talked with people on the boat who had relatives and affidavits for the U.S.A., but were going to Palestine instead.

Is this so hard to understand? They have been kicked around as Jews and now they want to live as Jews. Over and over again, I heard it said: "We want to build a Jewish country. . . . We are tired of putting our sweat and blood into places where we are not welcome. . . . We have wandered enough." These Jews want the right to live as a people, to build as a people, to make their contribution to the world as a people. Are their national aspirations any less worthy of respect than those of any other oppressed people?

I was impressed, on my underground voyage, with the vitality I found among these, my brethren from the East. What is the source of this vitality and strength? The source is twofold. The first lies in the Zionist idea, in this romantic dream of a Viennese journalist in the late nineteenth century, the dream of a Return. This has given them a goal, their lives a purpose, their shattered selves a focal point around which to reintegrate their personalities and to recover their moral health.

The second source of their strength is simpler. It is that lack of alternative to which I have already referred.

"For us," one of my friends had said to me on shipboard, "Palestine is the last stop. We can go no farther." They have nothing to lose, hardly life itself—for life for Jews in Poland and Rumania and Hungary today is too precarious to be worth much, and life in the DP camps is hardly life at all, but a kind of waiting day after day in an open grave, from which one may or may not arise.

Such people, in such a mood, are not easily defeated. They who knew the SS are not terrified by the British. They who saw the gas chambers are not frightened by a naval blockade. They are going to *Eretz*.

I say here what I said in private to Azzam Bey Pasha, head of the Arab League, over coffee in Cairo. I did not say it in defiance, for I respect Azzam Bey, and I would far rather deal with that Arab statesman and patriot on behalf of the Jews than with Ernest Bevin. I said it as a simple statement of fact when he asked what I thought of the current situation: *"Nothing will stop the people I traveled with from rebuilding a great Jewish community in Palestine."*

II

I came back convinced that the Jewish people can expect nothing whatsoever from the British government, except disappointment, betrayal, and attack. I say that with apologies to the good friends the cause of the DP's and of Palestine has in each of the three British parties in England and even among British officialdom in the Middle East.

I want to set down in all soberness the simple statement that the British Empire is now waging a war designed to smash what the Jews have accomplished in Palestine and to break the hearts of the homeless in the DP camps and elsewhere by shutting off their one hope—the so-called illegal immigration.

I say so-called illegal immigration because the only right Britain has to the control of Palestine and Trans-Jordan lies in a League of Nations mandate and a separate treaty with the United States giving Britain temporary trusteeship in order to establish a Jewish national home. To bar Jews from the Holy Land is to violate the mandate and the treaty.

I would not be reporting accurately if I left the impression that any such legalistic argument lies behind the

determined migration of my old comrades across dangerous frontiers and blockaded seas. The British Foreign
Office may consider this another bit of stubborn Jewish
foolishness, but Jews—who have long historical memories
—instinctively think of Palestine as a place in which they
have rights older than a League of Nations mandate, em-
bodied in a document which Christian Britain respects,
though sometimes only on Sunday.

When I was in Jerusalem, I was told in one of the best
informed sources in the Middle East that the British military had drawn up a three-part plan which was to culmi-
nate—if sufficient excuse could be found—in an offensive
operation designed to smash Jewish settlements and cities.
One high British military official told a Jewish leader
frankly—I assure the reader this is not just gossip—"The
world took the killing of six million Jews and if we have
to destroy half of Tel Aviv, the world will take that, too."

The British are too humane a people to send the Jews
of Europe to gas chambers as the Nazis did, but their government can be very cruel in an absent-minded and com-
placent way when the supposed needs of the Empire are
at stake. The British government doesn't intend to kill the
homeless Jews of Europe—it just wants to destroy their
hopes. But that amounts to the same thing in the end.
As one Jewish ex-Partisan said to me on shipboard, "The
Germans killed us. The British don't let us live."

The British are not playing a pro-Arab game. I have
heard the amused contempt with which British officials in
Cairo react to talk of Arab aspirations. The British are
trying to build an alliance with the Moslem upper classes

in the Middle East against the Soviet Union, and also
against France and the United States. They want to keep
the whole area under their control and they are prepared
to sacrifice not only the Jews but the Christian minorities
of the East in that program.

I am not making demagogic flourishes. I know how
fearful the Christian minorities in Egypt, the Lebanon,
and Iraq are of present British policy.

The Moslem upper class on the whole—with the exception of some far-sighted men—share with the British:

1. The phobia about the USSR.
2. Fear of unrest among the miserable Arab masses,
   and
3. Dislike for the modern ideas and methods
   brought to the ancient East by the returning
   Jews.

The British are shrewder than the pashas and the
effendis. The British realize the need for development in
the East. But development is now only possible with
American capital, and they want to keep the Middle East
as their private preserve. Development also would antag-
onize the reactionary ruling class elements who are the
only allies the British can muster. One distinguished British oriental expert said to me, "If we urge social reform
of the effendis, they will say 'what difference is there, then,
between you and the Bolsheviks?'"

The clue to this aspect of British policy is that instead
of asking for an American loan to develop the Jordan

Valley and similar water possibilities in Egypt, Syria, and Iraq, they are asking us to provide a $300,000,000 loan for the Arab potentates who rule those countries. There are no more corrupt rulers in the world today and the money will go straight into their private treasuries. This is the politics of *baksheesh*.

The British government wants the Middle East to remain an area of backwardness, a territory of "natives" and "native rulers" whom they can handle in the traditional way. They want Palestine to be their military base in the Middle East, and they offer freedom neither to the Arabs nor to the Jews. They who pride themselves on sportsmanship and gallantry are prepared to use overwhelming force —as they did when they ludicrously mobilized 5000 troops with tanks against the 160 villagers (50 of them children) in Sadoth Yam near Haifa.

I know the Jews of Palestine and I know how they must have chuckled at that unconscious tribute to their bravery and fighting power. The world will yet see that this is a struggle from which Britain will emerge with shame, but not with victory.

III

The exodus of Jews from Europe, of which I was an eye witness, is the greatest in the history of the Jewish people, greater than the migrations of the past out of Egypt and Spain. To tell its story properly one would need to be not a newspaper reporter, but an ancient Hebrew prophet. The journey was a journey for a Jeremiah. For it is a story which should be told as Parable and Warning.

The Jewish problem is a minor problem; Hitler left Bevin all too few. But what happens to them will be a portent. One need not believe in any divine retribution to see that the conditions which make it impossible for Jews to live in most of Central and Eastern Europe, and the conditions which block their aspiration for a return to their ancient homeland, are also the conditions which threaten mankind with new and quite possibly final disaster.

In that sense one need not be clairvoyant to see that history will exact a price for the treatment accorded the remnants of European Jewry. Unfortunately there is little comfort for the victims in apocalyptic perspectives.

In a sane and orderly world, the U.S.A., USSR, France, and Britain would join in an international development scheme for the Middle East and in a context of rising living standards provide ample room for the Jews in Palestine. I myself would like to see a bi-national Arab-Jewish state made of Palestine and Trans-Jordan, the whole to be part of a Middle Eastern Semitic Federation.

I would like to see a ten-year international trusteeship for Palestine in the course of which first through *consultative* and then using *representative* bodies, Jews and Arabs, Christians and Moslems would begin to work together as they do so successfully today in the half-Arab, half-Jewish municipality of Haifa.

After seeing Europe I am more than ever convinced

that Jews and Arabs can live together in peace. There is no such ill feeling in Palestine between Jew and Arab as exists in Czechoslovakia between Czech and Slovak, or in Yugoslavia between Croat and Serb.

I am also convinced that there isn't a chance of any such rational solution because the British don't want it, because it would set in motion a peaceful social revolution in the East, and because it would upset the potentates and pashas with whom the oil companies, American and British, do business.

I think the Jews must look to themselves and that they and those who are touched by their plight must put all their money and energies into the so-called illegal immigration. The only practical thing that can be done is to buy and man ships and with those ships to get the Jews out of Central and Eastern Europe.

What if the British catch most of the immigrants and send them to Cyprus? The answer is that Cyprus is only 180 miles from Palestine, that Jews are better off there than rotting morally in the DP camps, and that the job of the underground is to make their cruel blockade as costly and difficult as possible for the British.

This will be a crucial year for Jewry. There may be serious trouble in the camps, where morale is worse than ever. The British may widen offensive operations against Jewish settlements in Palestine. This is a war in which the lives and hopes of European Jewry and the accomplishments of the *Yishuv* in Palestine are at stake.

I believe that full support of the so-called illegal immigration is a moral obligation for world Jewry and a

Christian duty for its friends. I believe that the only hope lies in filling the waters of Palestine with so many illegal boats that the pressure on the British and the conscience of the world becomes unbearable.

And if those ships are illegal, so was the Boston Tea Party.

Acknowledgments

I want to thank: Ralph Ingersoll, the editor, and John P. Lewis, the managing editor, of *PM,* for letting me make this trip and for the instinctive and characteristic humanity and sympathy they have displayed on this, as on every fundamental issue; Miss Viola Young, for some hard and devoted editorial work on the book; David Zucker, of Parish Press, for making possible an extraordinarily swift publication; and on this job of writing, as in all else, my wife.

1946

Reflections and Meditations
Thirty Years After

PART I:
Confessions of a Jewish Dissident

—I. F. Stone
Washington, March 9, 1978

Abstractly speaking, I should be quite a popular person in the American Jewish community. I am a dissident. I am also, at a time when the search is on for moderate voices on the Palestine question, a moderate. And I proved my devotion to displaced persons in and out of the Middle East years ago. I have a medal to prove it, from the *Haganah*—the illegal Jewish army that fought what Prime Minister Begin calls the Jewish war of liberation and established the state of Israel in 1948.

Yet despite all these credentials I find myself—like many fellow American intellectuals, Jewish and non-Jewish—ostracized whenever I try to speak up on the Middle East. This demonstrates what slight changes in time and space can do to familiar categories. Dissidents, Jewish and non-Jewish, in the Soviet Union are—deservedly—heroes. They may be forced to circulate their views in *samizdat,* they may be dependent for circulation in their homeland on the type-writer and carbon paper. But at least they make the front pages of the American and world press, and the correspondents in Moscow hang on their words. Here at least their books are best-sellers.

But it is only rarely that we dissidents on the Middle East can enjoy a fleeting voice in the American press. Finding an American publishing house willing to publish a book that departs from the standard Israeli line is about as easy as selling a thoughtful exposition of atheism to the Osservatore Romano in Vatican City.

In this respect, our lot is worse than that of the Arabs. Even before Sadat's visit to Jerusalem made it fashionable, there were synagogues willing to invite Egyptian and even Palestinian Arabs, and occasionally an American of Arab origin to explain his viewpoint. Only a few days ago Mohammed Hakki, an able and eloquent Egyptian newspaperman who now works for his country's embassy here in Washington, was given a Sabbath forum and heard with courtesy at Adas Israel, one of the capital's most prestigious congregations.

But I have yet to hear of an American journalist of dissident views, Jewish or gentile, accorded similar treatment. I will not name them but there are top figures in the profession, with long records of championing Israel and the Jewish people, who complain bitterly in private that if they dare express one word of sympathy for Palestinian Arab refugees, they are flooded with Jewish hate-mail accusing them of anti-Semitism.

As for Jewish dissidents in America, we get the standard treatment. We are labeled "self-hating Jews." American Jewish intellectuals are lectured on what is stigmatized as their weakness for "universalism." One distinguished academic was summoned to an Israeli consulate for a scolding and put into deep freeze by colleagues for advocating a generous peace policy toward the Palestinian Arabs. We are asked why we cannot be narrow ethnics, suspicious of any breed but our own. Isaiah is out of fashion.

Gentile dissidents are generally treated simply as anti-Semites, no matter how often they have demonstrated friendship for Israel and the Jews in the past. A pro-Israel Republican senator, many of whose closest aides are Jewish, suddenly found himself treated as an enemy by the organized Jewish community in his state because on a trip to the Middle East he had ventured some expression of sympathy for the Arabs, too.

Even the Quakers are on the blacklist; they have demonstrated that the peacemakers may be blessed in heaven but they have a hard time on earth. At their Mideast peace conference in Washington last summer they were picketed by Jewish organizations. The State Department cooperated by denying a visa to a Palestinian moderate scheduled to speak there. (The Jewish dissidents of Breira, meeting at the same 4-H Club headquarters in Chevy Chase a week later, got worse treatment: the Jewish Defense League invaded the meeting, breaking up furniture and tearing up membership lists.)

On the Middle East, freedom of debate is not encouraged. Much ill will has been piled up, though not publicly expressed, in Congress, the government, and the press by the steamroller tactics of the hard-liners.

My trouble originally began with my weakness for refugees. In the spring of 1946 I was the first reporter to travel with "displaced persons" (as they were then called) out of the Nazi camps from Poland to Palestine through the British blockade. After making that trip, I found myself a hero in the American Jewish community, a speaker at more than one national convention of Hadassah. I can even remember being trotted out by the Zionists to persuade the (then) Uncle Toms of the American Jewish Committee to overcome their fears of identifying with the Zionist cause.

Now their publication, *Commentary,* has become the principal pillory for Americans who dissent from the Israeli hard line. In the past twenty-five years I have been asked to speak in a synagogue only once, and I won't name it lest I again embarrass its rabbi, for then I made the mistake of asking sympathy for Arab refugees as well. I remember, as if it were yesterday, the horror of statelessness in the thirties for those who fled Fascist and Nazi oppression. I feel for the scattered Palestinians who would like a state and a passport too.

My first taste of being a dissident came quite early. When I got back from my illegal trip, my series "Underground to Palestine," in the New York newspaper *PM,* was an instant success. It pushed circulation to a high point which, if maintained, might have saved Ralph Ingersoll's unique experiment in publishing a newspaper without advertising. I traveled with some of the most wonderful people I have ever met, both passengers and crew—including survivors of the death camps and the handful of American-Jewish sailors who volunteered to man the ships taking them to Palestine.

The story of their lives and adventures stirred sympathy for the Zionist cause among Jews and non-Jews alike. When publication in book form was planned, I was taken to lunch by friends in the Zionist movement, including a partner in one of the topmost advertising firms in America. They outlined a $25,000 advertising campaign to put the book across. But then came the awkward moment.

There was one sentence, I was told, just a sentence or so, that had to come out. I asked what that was. It was the sentence in which I suggested a bi-national solution, a state whose constitution would recognize, irrespective of shifting majorities, the presence of two peoples, two nations, Arab and Jewish, within Palestine, with two official languages, Arabic and Hebrew, which are now indeed the two official languages in the state of Israel.

That position may sound like dreadful heresy today. It was not that far out in 1946, a year before the United Nations decided to partition the country between two states, Arab and Jewish, with economic and other links between them. At that time the Hashomer Hatzair, the Left Zionists, an important sector of the Zionist movement then as now, had long advocated a bi-national solution. In addition I then suggested that the bi-national state be established in the whole of Palestine, as it was before 1922. It was then that the British carved out a new kingdom across the Jordan for the Hashemite dynasty, after the Saudi family drove them out of Mecca and established their fierce fundamentalist Wahabi state, where barbarous penalties straight out of the Bible are still imposed for adultery and theft. This was the consolation prize for Britain's friend, King Abdullah.

I refused to take this passage out. "My boss, Ralph Ingersoll," I said, "allowed me to make the three-month trip at considerable sacrifice for the paper. He did not tell me what to write. It was printed that way in *PM*. He would have a low opinion of me, quite rightly, if I submitted to such censorship for the sake of an advertising campaign." That ended the luncheon, and in a way, the book. It was in effect boycotted.

But two years later the book was translated into Hebrew with the offending passage intact, though the translator was a leading member of the Mapai, the dominant party in Zionism and as deeply opposed as my interlocutors in America to a bi-national solution. And as the 1948 war approached, copies of the book were given out to *sabras,* or native-born Palestinian Jews, in the armed forces to help them understand how Jews had suffered and how some had survived the Holocaust.

As so often since, dissent frowned upon in the United States was allowed in Israel, so long as it was published in Hebrew. To this day few American Jews realize how much free debate goes on in the Hebrew press and in Hebrew book publishing there. The language barrier makes possible a most useful little Iron Curtain behind which American Jews can be herded into supporting the hard official line.

Arabs who read Hebrew, and many do, have free access

to this debate, but we do not. Very little of Israeli debate, either in the press or the Knesset, filters through to the American public. Few American correspondents know Hebrew, and only the official statements are easily available in English. Consequently the coverage of the last Knesset session, after Sadat's walkout from the peace talks, might just as well have been coverage of a rubber-stamp parliament in any Third World dictatorship. None of the dissenting voices was reported. All we got was what Begin said.

This failure to report Israeli debate is a great obstacle to wise decision making here. Many in Israel, too, feel that it is not anti-Semitic to believe that a generous attitude toward the Palestinian Arabs may be a better safeguard of Israel's future than the niggardly something-for-nothing response of the hard-liners.

Moderates in Israel look to the leaders of the American Jewish community for leverage against the hard-liners, and the timid doves of the Jewish establishment here look to opinion in Israel for support; but communication between them is blocked off, and the result is a rigid, monolithic policy totally unsuited to the great opportunities opened up by Sadat's courageous initiative.

Many here in the United States must have felt appalled at Sadat's reception in Jerusalem. I knew Chaim Weizmann, and he was not only a masterly diplomat but could bring something of the poet to political discourse. Had he still been alive and the president of Israel, he would have risen to the occasion with a magnanimous gesture and a healing phrase. But all Sadat got from Begin was a warmed-over UJA speech. Begin's response made me blush.

Quite a few people in Israel shared that same feeling of disappointment over Begin's response to the Sadat visit, but you would hardly guess it from press coverage here. *Ma'ariv,* the biggest newspaper in Israel, ran a long interview covering more than one full page with the deputy prime minister, Yigal Yadin, taking issue with Begin after the Sadat meeting and calling for a more flexible policy. To have the deputy prime minister disagree publicly with the prime minister was a major political story, but so far as I know the only paper in this country that printed the deputy prime minister's statement was the Washington *Star* (December 4). I didn't see it even mentioned elsewhere. The headline in *Ma'ariv* indicated the divergence between Begin and his deputy prime minister: "The Moment of Truth Comes and Israel Will Have to State Its Willingness for Territorial Concessions in Judea and Samaria [the West Bank] Or Else There Will Be No Peace."

One of the many other unreported voices of dissent was that of G. Schocken, editor of Israel's most respected paper, *Ha'aretz,* who expressed his disagreement with Begin in an unusual signed editorial. The Knesset debate then too was meagerly reported. When I tried to get the Israeli *Congressional Record (Divrei Ha Knesset)* from the Israeli desk of the State Department, I was told after the usual bureaucratic indifference that the latest copies the State Department had were a few issues from the year 1965!

Yet it would help the administration to resist the monolithic hard-liners if the American Congress and public were made more aware of dissent in Israel. The most striking recent example was the editorial in the Jerusalem *Post* (international edition of January 24) on Sadat's action in breaking off the peace talks. While expressing regret over the "tougher line" taken by Sadat in his speech recalling his negotiators from Jerusalem, the *Post* said:

> His criticism about Israel's handling of the talks and some of the public statements made here should however also lead to some self-review in Jerusalem. For certainly Sadat seemed to have every right to wonder about Israel's intentions when bulldozers in Sinai, replete with fanfare, suddenly materialized while he was supposedly gaining agreement about Israeli withdrawal, and when Israeli rhetoric countered a commitment to desist from polemics.

The Jerusalem *Post* has long been the distinguished English voice of the Israeli community. Its scarcely veiled rebuke to Begin is quite different from the unrestrained condemnation in this country of Sadat by such figures as Rabbi Alexander M. Schindler, chairman of the Conference of Presidents of Major Jewish Organizations. He said Sadat's "impatience conveys the impression that you disdain the negotiating process in its entirety" (*The New York Times,* January 30).

I was brought up to believe that a fundamental pillar of any stable political situation is—in that historic American phrase—"the consent of the governed." How can there be a stable, secure relationship between Israel and the Palestinian Arabs, both those on the West Bank and those stateless in the Palestinian Diaspora, without their consultation and consent?

To impose the kind of "self-rule" Begin envisages on the Palestinians is to push Israel into an endless sea of troubles. How do you make sure the people they elect to office are not secretly sympathizers with the PLO, or not "moderate" enough to suit Israel, Hussein, or Carter?

Do you cross-examine candidates in advance to make sure they're satisfactory? Do you open their mail, bug their phones, and police their social contacts to make sure they stay that way? And how much respect will Palestinians have for this variety of "self-rulers"?

The frown of the occupying power or of foreign statesmen may defeat itself by conferring legitimacy. When Carter on the eve of his recent trip abroad "ruled out" the PLO in advance, he invited embarrassing questions. If negotiations are to be limited to "moderates," does that rule out Begin and the Likud too? If the Palestinians are to have self-rule, what gives Carter the right to cast the first ballot?

All else becomes negotiable if the principle of self-determination is recognized. A transition period in which old fears are allayed and both sides can settle down comfortably into coexistence has much to be said for it. But not if "self-rule" is a counterfeit and "transition" invites Gush Emunim to expand its settlements and erode a future Palestinian state even before it is born.

The latest warning signal was the news that a new West Bank settlement is being established in Shiloh, despite Begin's promise to Carter, on the novel plea that this is only an "archeological" settlement. If archeology can excuse new settlements, and Gush Emunim disguise itself as a mere band of eager beaver Schliemanns, no place is safe. There is no spot in the Holy Land where some antiquity cannot be dug up. But the administration is so timorous that Carter's note of protest to Begin, instead of being given full publicity, was leaked to James Reston's column in *The New York*

Times, Sunday, January 29, as if the White House were afraid to raise its voice directly.

Washington has not even reacted to Dayan's remark in a recent Knesset debate that under "self-rule" the Israeli army would have the right not only to protect Jewish settlements on the West Bank but to enforce further land acquisition by Jews. Such threats hardly serve the cause of security and stability for Israel and the Middle East.

History over and over again has proven magnanimity a better safeguard than myopic military thinking. Those who wish to see the case for alternative policies in the precarious Middle East negotiations should read the thoughtful analyses by two Israeli doves in recent interviews here, which deserve far wider attention than they have received. One was the interview with Mattityahu Peled in the February 23 issue of *The New York Review of Books,* and the other with Arie Eliav in the December 24 *Nation* and (a longer version) in the January–February issue of *Worldview* magazine. Both these Israelis are seasoned by experience. Peled was a major general in the Israeli armed forces and Eliav was secretary general in 1970 to 1972 of Israel's then ruling Labor Party. But both, despite their past eminence, now that they are dissidents are in danger of being reduced to non-persons. They get little attention in the press and television.

How can wise solutions be reached, and the opportunity for peace rescued, when such dissident voices are hardly heard here above a whisper in what passes for debate on the Middle East? How can we talk of human rights and ignore them for the Palestinian Arabs? How can Israel talk of the

Jewish right to a homeland and deny one to the Palestinians? How can there be peace without some measure of justice?

PART II:
The Other Zionism

The main current of Zionism has always nourished itself on the illusion that the Jews were "a people without a land" returning to "a land without a people." But there was from the beginning of the movement another Zionism, now almost forgotten, except by scholars, which was prepared, from the deepest ethical motives, to face up to the reality that Palestine was not an empty land but contained another and kindred people. They were a lonely handful then, and a lonelier one now, when the pendulum of power has swung to the far right, to the ultra-nationalists, with their old leader, Menachem Begin, in office.

Perhaps never more than now has this Other Zionism seemed more like a voice in the political wilderness, but the time may be coming when more and more Israelis and Jews will wish these voices had been heard, and when their message will take on renewed life and meaning if there is to be peace and Israel is to survive.

In their time, the spokesmen for this Other Zionism were not obscure and peripheral figures, but among the most resplendent names in the history of the Return. They were among the greatest of the thinkers and the pioneers who prepared the way for the reestablishment of Israel. One of them, Ahad Ha Am, was the foremost philosopher to take part in the rebirth of Hebrew as a living language in our time. Among these Other Zionists was his disciple, the San Francisco-born American rabbi Judah L. Magnes, who emigrated to Palestine in 1922. His monumental achievement was in establishing the Hebrew University in Jerusalem; he became its chancellor when it opened in 1925 and served as its first president until his death in 1948.

Ahad Ha Am, a Russian Jewish intellectual, played a role in obtaining the Balfour Declaration by which the British government pledged itself in 1917 to establish in Palestine "a national home for the Jewish people." Ahad Ha Am was also one of the few in the Zionist movement who stressed the parallel obligation expressed in the Declaration, "that nothing shall be done which may prejudice the civil and religious rights of existing non-Jewish communities in Palestine." Ahad Ha Am called himself a "cultural Zionist." He wanted the political aims of Zionism limited, as his biography in the *Encyclopaedia Judaica* expresses it, by "consideration for the national rights of the Palestinian Arabs." This was a note rarely if ever struck by the spokesmen for main-line Zionism. These regarded the pledge to the Palestinian Arabs as a kind of British imperialist trick and insisted on reading the Balfour Declaration as a promise not to create a Jewish national home *in* Palestine but to turn all Palestine into a Jewish state.

Four years after the Balfour Declaration was promulgated, Ahad Ha Am expanded his views on it in a preface to the Berlin edition of his book, *At the Cross Ways*. He wrote then that the historical right of the Jewish people to a national home in Palestine "does not invalidate the right of the rest of the land's inhabitants." He recognized that they have "a genuine right to the land due to generations of

residence and work upon it." For them "too," Ahad Ha Am
went on, "this country is a national home and they have the
right to develop their national potentialities to the utter-
most." He felt that this "makes Palestine into a common
possession of different peoples."

This was why, Ahad Ha Am explained, the British government "promised to facilitate the establishment in Palestine of a National Home for the Jewish people and not, as
was proposed to it, the reconstruction of Palestine as the
National Home for the Jewish people." Ahad Ha Am said
the purpose of the Balfour Declaration was two-fold: (1)
to establish a Jewish National Home there, but (2) also to
deny "any right to deprive the present inhabitants of their
rights" and any intention "of making the Jewish people
the sole ruler of the country."*

Ahad Ha Am died in 1927. But his younger American
disciple, Magnes, followed in his footsteps. He made a life-
long effort to bring Arabs and Jews together, and to work
for a bi-national state in which the national rights and aspirations of both peoples would be safeguarded by fundamental constitutional guarantees. In such a state the constitution,
regardless of which was at any time the majority, would
recognize two nations within the one state, with full rights
to cultural autonomy, fostered by two official languages,
Arabic and Hebrew.

The considerations that led Magnes all his life to espouse
this view were movingly set forth in his address opening
the Hebrew University in Jerusalem for its 1929–30 academic year. This old address reads with fresh meaning and

*From an English translation by Judah L. Magnes in his own book,
Like All the Nations?, published in Jerusalem in 1930, p. 65.

pathos in the wake of the South Lebanese invasion and the use by the Israeli army of cluster bombs against the civilian population. "One of the greatest cultural duties of the Jewish people," Magnes said then, "is the attempt to enter the Promised Land, not by means of conquest as Joshua, but through peaceful and cultural means, through hard work, sacrifices, love and with a decision not to do anything which cannot be justified before the world conscience."

There was much of the same spirit in the writings and example of an earlier pioneer, A. D. Gordon, who died in 1922, the year Magnes first settled in Palestine. Gordon was a Tolstoyan Zionist who left his family in Russia in 1904 to live in Palestine. He believed that the Jews could reestablish a nation in Palestine only if they began to build it, literally, with their own hands. Though he was already forty-eight years of age when he emigrated, and a writer and philosopher hitherto unused to physical labor, he set out to live as he believed. "He worked," says his biography in the *Encyclopaedia Judaica,* "as a manual laborer in the vineyards and orange groves of Petah Tikvah and Rishon le-Zion"—two of the oldest Jewish farming settlements in Palestine—"and, after 1912, in various villages in Galilee, suffering all the tribulations of the pioneers: malaria, unemployment, hunger and insecurity." He lies buried near the villages among which he worked and I remember, on my first visit to Palestine in 1945, standing beside his grave under the willows in the rustic peace of the little cemetery outside Degania where the Jordan reemerges from the sea of Galilee. Gordon is perhaps the most inspiring single figure among all the early pioneers, and the younger people beside whom he worked felt his saintly quality.

Gordon was a secular mystic, a nationalist who was also a universalist. This is how he himself saw the mission of the nation he helped to resurrect. "We were the first to proclaim," Gordon wrote of the Jews, "that man is created in the image of God. We must go further and say: the nation must be created in the image of God. Not because we are better than others, but because we have borne upon our shoulders and suffered all which calls for this. It is by paying the price of torments the like of which the world has never known"—the Holocaust was still beyond even his vision—"that we have won the right to be the first in this work of creation."

In Gordon's opinion the test, the crucial test, of the Jews would be their attitude toward the Arabs. "Our attitude toward them," he wrote, "must be one of humanity, of moral courage which remains on the highest plane, even if the behavior of the other side is not all that is desired. Indeed," he concluded, "their hostility is all the more reason for our humanity."

Gordon's approach was rather singular. In an age of socialism, nationalism, and skepticism, his first consideration was the redemption of the individual. He once wrote, "Our road leads to nature through the medium of physical labor." Hence his has been called "the religion of labor." He felt, as a biographer put it, that "God cannot be known, but he can be experienced and lived." He felt that the transformation of society must begin with the transformation of the individual, and he rejected utilitarianism and Marxism. For Gordon, though a nationalist, the nation was "the intermediary between the individual and humanity as a whole." In his view, "each and every nation must see itself

as a unit responsible for the fate of humanity and for the
attainment of universal justice." From this it followed that
"the relationship between the Jews and the Arabs in Palestine was important because if the Jews were to recreate
their nation as a just nation this could not be done on the
basis of injustice." The Jews, in his view, had a right to return "to Palestine and become once again a part of it, but
the Arabs were part of it, too."* Gordon believed, as his
biographer in the *Encyclopaedia Judaica* expresses it, that
"a people incarnate humanity only to the extent to which
it obeys the moral law."

In this, Gordon saw eye to eye with the Prophets and
with Ahad Ha Am. For Gordon, the Arab problem was
central. He recognized that the Arabs were "a living nation, though not a free one" (he was writing in 1919, remember), and that like it or not they would be "partners
with us in the political and social life" of the country. He
saw Arab-Jewish relations as "a great moment" because
"here we have the first lesson and the first practical exercise
in the life of brotherhood between nations." He saw this as
an essential test "in every one of us," that is, the Jews, "in-
dividually," and concluded that "if we shall aim at being
more human, more alive, we will find the correct relation-
ships to man and the nations in general and to the Arabs in
particular." † The test of Jewish humanity was to be in the
Jewish attitude toward the Arabs.

---

*Gordon, as summarized by Susan Lee Hattis in her doctoral thesis at
the University of Geneva, *The Bi-National Idea in Palestine During
Mandatory Times* (Jerusalem: Shikmona Publishing Company, 1970).

†Translated from the Hebrew by Hattis, *op. cit.,* from pp. 242 and
245 of the volume on The Nation and Work, in the *Collected Works
of Aharon David Gordon* (Jerusalem: Zionist Publications, 1952–4).

Nor did Gordon see this relationship purely in terms of mystic vision. He translated it into terms of the land question, fearing the coming dispossession of the Arab peasant.

In 1922, when drafting statues for the guidance of Zionist labor settlements, he included a provision long forgotten. "Wherever settlements are founded," Gordon advised,

> a specific share of the land must be assigned to the Arabs from the outset. The distribution of sites should be equitable so that not only the welfare of the Jewish settler but equally that of the resident Arabs will be safeguarded. The settlement has the moral obligation to assist the Arabs in any way it can. This is the only proper and fruitful way to establish good neighborly relations with the Arabs.*

This may have seemed quixotic at the time and soon became a dead letter, but it held the key to fraternity and peace.

A similar message came from a very different sector of European Jewry, from the German-Jewish philosopher Martin Buber. He too was influenced by Ahad Ha Am. He became a Zionist as early as 1898, but for him Zionism was to be different from all other nationalisms. It was to be *Der Heilige Weg,* the Holy Way. This was the title of a book he published in 1919 in his native Germany. In it he espoused a "Hebrew humanism." He too saw relations with the Arabs as crucial. In his writings he "emphasized"—as his biographer in the *Encyclopaedia Judaica* phrased it—"that Zionism should address itself to the needs of the Arabs." He set forth the germ of the idea of a bi-national state as early as 1921, in a proposal to the Zionist Congress held that year. He wanted the Congress officially to proclaim "its desire to

---

*Quoted from *Studies in Nationalism, Judaism and Universalism,* edited by Raphael Loewe (London: Routledge & Kegan Paul, 1966).

live in peace and brotherhood with the Arab people and to develop the common homeland into a republic in which both peoples will have the possibility of free development."

After Hitler came to power in 1933, Buber stayed on in Germany for five terrifying years, as long as he could help maintain the morale of his fellow Jews. When the new regime closed the doors of German universities to "non-Aryans," Buber helped to organize and became the head of a communal organization to provide higher education for German-Jewish youth. He made himself the focus of a spiritual resistance by traveling about the country, lecturing to the Jewish communities. In 1935, when the régime forbade him to speak at Jewish gatherings, he found a way through the Quakers to evade that order. The German Friends invited him to speak at their meetings, which were open to all, including Jews. This too was soon forbidden. In 1938 Buber emigrated to Palestine. There I once had the privilege of speaking with him after the war. He had the aura of a Hebrew prophet.

In Palestine Buber made the search for Arab-Jewish friendship one of his main concerns. Even after the outbreak of the first Arab-Jewish war in 1948, Buber "called for a harnessing of nationalistic impulses and a solution based on compromise between the two peoples." He was a close friend of Magnes's and taught at the Hebrew University until his death in 1965. His lovely German style makes his works among the treasures of German literature, and he belongs to the Other Germany as well as to the Other Zionism.

One of the earliest figures in the Other Zionism was Moshe Smilansky (1874–1953). The son of a tenant farmer near Kiev in Russia, Smilansky emigrated to Palestine in 1890. He was active as a farmer, writer, and Zionist. He too was among the bi-nationalists. He opposed the movement to restrict employment in Jewish colonies and fields to Jewish labor. He had the distinction of being the first modern Hebrew writer to write about the Arabs among whom he settled. Under the pen name of Hawaja Mussa, he published amiable short stories about Arab life before World War I. These stories, "the first of their kind in Jewish literature," says the *Encyclopaedia Judaica,* revealed "to the Jewish reader a new world—exotic, colorful, throbbing with its own rich humanity."

A similar figure, out of that same pioneering generation, was the agronomist Hayim Kalwariski-Margolis, a warm and ebullient man, whom I met on my first visit to Palestine in 1945; his was the only Jewish home in which I encountered Arab intellectuals. By 1945 he had already spent fifty years in Palestine devoted to Jewish resettlement and Arab-Jewish friendship. After leaving his native village in Russian Poland, Kalwariski prepared himself for life in Palestine by studying agronomy in France at the University of Montpellier. Upon his graduation in 1895 he emigrated to the Holy Land. There he became a teacher at the new Mikve Israel Agricultural School, the first of its kind in Palestine.

Many of the earliest and most famous pre-World War I settlements in Galilee owe much to Kalwariski for their foundation and survival. To protect these colonies, Kalwariski helped to organize the legendary *Ha-Shomer,* the Jewish armed watchmen's organization, from which the *Haganah,* the underground self-defense force of the Jewish community, ultimately developed. He also pioneered in the search for better relations with their Arab neighbors. He persuaded the Baron Edmond de Rothschild to establish a Hebrew-Arab school, the first of its kind, for the children of the Arab village of Ja'uni near the Jewish village of Rosh Pina in Galilee.

Kalwariski played a part in a whole series of attempts to establish amicable relations between the rising forces of Arab and Jewish nationalism. As early as 1913 he arranged meetings in Damascus and Beirut between the famous Zionist leader Nahum Sokolow and Arab nationalists. After World War I, King Feisal I, who had led the Arab revolt against the Turks, paid Kalwariski an unusual tribute. Kalwariski was invited by the newly crowned king in Damascus and the presidium of the All-Syrian Congress "to suggest proposals for the regulation of Jewish-Arab relations in Palestine." In 1922 Kalwariski participated in Arab-Jewish negotiations in Cairo, which were discontinued "because of the opposition of the British government." (Ernest Bevin, as foreign minister, similarly upset plans for a secret meeting in Cairo after World War II at which the Egyptians hoped to mediate the Arab-Jewish conflict in Palestine. Bevin aborted the meetings by threatening to make it public and so embarrass the Arab participants.)

In those years Kalwariski was not acting merely as an unauthorized Zionist heretic. He was one of the three Jewish members of the Arab-Jewish Advisory Council set up for Palestine by the first British High Commissioner, Sir Herbert Samuel, under the post-World War I British mandatory government of Palestine established by the League of Nations. Kalwariski also served on the executive of the

Va'ad Le'umi, or National Council, which was a kind of unofficial governing body of the Palestinian Jewish community between the two world wars. From 1923 to 1927 he directed the Office of Arab Affairs of the Zionist Executive. In 1929, after the Arab uprising in that year, he was appointed head of the combined office set up by the Jewish Agency and the Va'ad Le'umi to deal with Arab-Jewish tensions.

Kalwariski did not limit his activities to these official Zionist bodies. He was a leading figure in a series of maverick organizations established in the twenties, thirties, and forties to bring about Arab-Jewish reconciliation. These all, in one form or another, advocated a bi-national state.* Though these were all politically marginal movements, with little impact on majority opinion, they attracted many of the best minds and most illustrious intellectuals of the Jewish community. The earliest was the Berit Shalom (Covenant of Peace). It was formed in 1925 by such leading pioneers and intellectuals as Arthur Ruppin, Hans Kohn, Gershom Scholem—now the leading authority on Jewish mysticism—and Kalwariski. This was the first organization to call for the establishment of a bi-national state in Palestine and it was bitterly attacked by most of the Zionist parties, especially by the right-wing Revisionist Zionist party to which Prime Minister Begin belongs. Berit Shalom was attacked as "defeatist," but the attacks, as is usual in controversy, evaded the point—

---

*I want to acknowledge my debt to Ms. Hattis and to recommend her book, already cited, for those who wish a fuller understanding of the bi-national movement. The book is the only one of its kind and it is written with a sympathetic and compassionate objectivity.

Berit Shalom had no ideology; bi-nationalism, they said, is not the ideal but the reality, and if this reality is not grasped Zionism will fail. They were not defeatists who were ready to make any concession for the achievement of peace, they simply realized that the Arabs were justified in fearing a Zionism which spoke in terms of a Jewish majority and a Jewish state. Their belief was that one need not be a maximalist, i.e., demand mass immigration and a state, to be a faithful Zionist. . . . What was vital was a recognition that both nations were in Palestine as of right.*

The Berit Shalom lasted until the early thirties. It was succeeded by three similar organizations: Kedma Mizrachi (Forward to the East) in the thirties; the League of Arab-Jewish Rapprochement, established in 1939; and then in 1942 by the last and most important bi-nationalist group, Ihud, which means unity in Hebrew, and here denotes unity with the Arabs. Kalwariski played a leading role in all these organizations.

These Jewish bi-nationalist groups, as their Zionist adversaries derisively pointed out, rarely if ever attracted Arab support. But the League of Arab-Jewish Rapprochement achieved a breakthrough in 1946. It came in Haifa, one of the three major cities of Palestine. The scene was significant. It could not have come in Jerusalem, where Arabs and Jews lived apart, or in Tel Aviv, which was all Jewish. But in Haifa the two communities had over the years achieved a bi-national form of government which was a miniature of what a bi-national Palestine could have been. The two peoples rotated the municipal offices between them. When the

---

*Hattis, *op. cit.*, p. 46.

mayor was an Arab, the vice mayor was a Jew, and vice versa. There in 1946 a leading Arab intellectual declared himself for a bi-national Palestine.

This maverick, Fauzi Darwish el-Husseini, was a member of the most influential Arab clan in Palestine, the Husseinis. He was a cousin of the Mufti of Jerusalem, Hajj Amin el-Husseini, the bitterest opponent of Zionism in his time. The Mufti went over to the Axis in World War II. But his cousin, at a public meeting in Haifa in 1946, expressed his readiness for Arab-Jewish cooperation. He said the obstacles were great but that there was a way. He called for an Arab-Jewish agreement, under the auspices of the United Nations, for a "bi-national independent Palestine," which would in turn link itself by "an alliance with the Arab neighboring countries."*

Fauzi amplified his views in a talk before an Arab-Jewish gathering in the home of Kalwariski a few days later. Fauzi said he had taken part in the Arab uprising of 1929 as a follower of his cousin, the Mufti, but had begun to realize "that this road has no purpose. Experience has proven," Fauzi went on, "that the official policy of both sides brings only damage and suffering to both." He said that in Palestine "the Jews and Arabs once lived in friendship and cooperation," and added that "there are Jews and Arabs from the older generation who nursed from the same mother." He said: "The imperialist policy plays with us both, with the Arabs and the Jews, and there is no other way except unity and working hand in hand."

---

*From the text as printed July 25, 1946, in the Hebrew daily *Al Ha Mishmar,* organ of the then bi-nationalist Hashomer Hatzair wing of the Zionist movement; translated at p. 303 of Hattis, *op. cit.*

Fauzi el-Husseini stressed that the moderates must organize. "A club must be set up immediately in Jerusalem to acquire friends, to begin producing a written organ, to visit other cities for propaganda and making ties." An Arab organization was formed called the Falastin al-Jedida (the New Palestine) and on November 11, 1946, five of its leading members signed an agreement with the League for Jewish-Arab Rapprochement and Cooperation. The two sides agreed to "full cooperation between the two nations in all fields on the basis of political equality between the two nations in Palestine as a means to obtaining the independence of the country . . . and the joining of the shared and independent Palestine in an alliance with the neighboring countries in the future." They even reached agreement on the thorniest problem of all—Jewish immigration. This was to be regulated "according to the absorptive capacity of the country."*

But this at first promising beginning was brought to an end twelve days later when Fauzi Darwish el-Husseini was murdered by unknown Arab nationalists. Never before (or since) had a Palestinian Arab leader dared openly to negotiate with the Jews and sign an agreement with them. Another cousin, Jamal Husseini, a leader of the Arab anti-Zionists, was quoted in the Egyptian paper *Akbar al Yom* as saying a few days after Fauzi's death, "My cousin stumbled and has received his proper punishment." According to one informed source, all other Arabs who had joined with him "were murdered by Arab extremists, one after the

---

*This and the preceding quotation were taken by Hattis from pp. 330 and 328 of Aharon Cohen's *Israel and the Arab World,* Sifriyat Poalim, Israel—the publishing house of the Kibbutz Haartzi section of the Zionist movement, which was bi-nationalist until 1948.

other."* How much agony could have been spared both peoples had Fauzi succeeded. Four Arab-Jewish wars would have been prevented. Who knows how many more will be fought before both sides see the inescapable choice between coexistence and mutual extinction?

Looking back, the basic problem between the two nationalisms was so acute that it would have been miraculous if the moderates had won out and resolved the issue peacefully. The basic question was Jewish immigration, which grew so rapidly after the rise of Hitler to power in 1933 that the Arabs feared—quite rightly, as it turned out—that they might soon be swamped and become a minority in what they regarded as their own land. They protested that they were being asked to pay the price for persecution of the Jews in Nazi Germany and in Eastern Europe. But from the Zionist point of view, immigration with the rise of Hitler had become a life-or-death question for the Jewish people.

Even before World War II, it became clear that many millions of Jews—indeed the 6 million who died in the Holocaust—could be saved only by being moved out of Europe before Hitler unleashed the war. The case was stated with passionate eloquence and prophetic vision by the poet Vladimir Jabotinsky, founding father of the Revisionists, the extreme nationalist right wing of the Zionist movement, in his testimony in 1937 before the Royal Commission in London set up under the chairman-

---

*Quoted in Norman Bentwich's article on Ihud in the *Encyclopaedia of Zionism and Israel*. Bentwich was at one time attorney general of the British mandatory government of Palestine, and sympathetic to the bi-nationalists. But his statement that Fauzi and his group were actually members of Ihud is not confirmed in Ms. Hattis's book.

ship of Lord Peel to investigate the Arab uprising of 1936.
Jabotinsky, speaking more truly than he could have known,
said the Jews in Central and Eastern Europe were "facing
an elemental calamity, a kind of social earthquake." Jabotinsky despaired of "really bringing before you a picture of
what that Jewish hell looks like." But, he said, "we have
got to save millions." The number might be "one-third of
the Jewish race, half of the Jewish race, or a quarter of the
Jewish race." And he recognized that "if the process of
evacuation is allowed to develop, as it ought to be allowed
to develop, there will soon be reached a moment when the
Jews will become a majority in Palestine."

This, of course, is what the Arabs feared and this was the
root cause of the Arab uprising that the Peel Commission
was set up to investigate. "I have the profoundest feeling
for the Arab case," Jabotinsky told the commission. But,
he added, "no tribunal has ever had the luck of trying a case
where all the justice was on the side of one party and the
other party had no case whatsoever." He thought the de-
termining consideration should be "the decisive terrible
balance of Need." He said there was no question of "ousting
the Arabs," but that Palestine "on both sides of the Jordan"
could hold many millions more of both Jews and Arabs.
He asked for a Jewish state, with rights of unlimited immigration, and argued that the Arabs already had several
national states and soon were to have many more.* This,
in substance, has remained the basic argument of the main-
line Zionists to this day. The Palestinian Arabs, in effect,
were to bear the burden of the crisis created by Hitler and
the unwillingness of the western powers, including the

---

*The full text of his moving appeal may be found in Arthur Hertz-
berg's *The Zionist Idea* (New York: Atheneum Publishers, 1969).

256

United States, to open their doors in time to the doomed masses of European Jewry.

The majority elements in Zionism finally adopted the Jewish state demand of the right-wing revisionists in December 1942, at the Biltmore Conference in New York. Even then, as the article on the Biltmore Program in the *Encyclopaedia of Zionism and Israel* explains, "Non-Zionist groups such as the American Jewish Committee regarded the Biltmore Program as a victory for the 'extreme' Zionist position, since it called for an independent Jewish Palestine rather than the mere lifting of barriers to future Jewish immigration." But only a Jewish state would allow unlimited immigration of Jews: this was the dilemma. At the time the Biltmore Program was adopted, the Holocaust was still a well-kept secret. The first leak to the outside world, according to Raul Hilberg's monumental and heartbreaking account, *The Destruction of the European Jews*,* was picked up by a Swedish diplomat on the Warsaw-Berlin express from a talkative Nazi official in the summer of 1942. But his report was kept secret by his own government. The full dimensions of the catastrophe were not "even imagined," Ms. Hattis writes of the Biltmore Conference; "and most Zionists were thinking and speaking in terms of millions of Jewish refugees after the war."†

Even so, resistance to a Jewish state was still a powerful undercurrent in the movement. The vote at the Biltmore was 21 to 4 for the new program. The four negative votes were cast by Hashomer Hatzair, the Marxist Zionists, who

---

* (Chicago: Quadrangle Books, 1961), p. 622.
†*Op. cit.,* pp. 249–50.

called instead for a bi-nationalist Palestine. They argued
that the alternative to bi-nationalism would be partition,
and partition would mean war with the Arabs. Events soon
proved they were right.

Four months before the Biltmore Conference, a group
of Zionist dissidents, among them two American Jews,
Judah Magnes and Henrietta Szold, organized Ihud
(Unity), an organization to establish friendly contact with
the Arabs and work for a bi-national solution. Magnes testi-
fied for Ihud in 1947 before the United Nations Special
Committee on Palestine in favor of a bi-national state. After
the United Nations had voted for the partition of Palestine
between an Arab and a Jewish state, with economic and
other links between them, Magnes pressed for the establishment of a Semitic Confederation, including Israel, as a
means of preventing the war he saw would result. Again, he
was unsuccessful. With the 1948 war and the establishment
of a Jewish state, the bi-national movement came to an end;
but not the Other Zionism, which continued to struggle for
justice to the Arabs in Israel, as later in the occupied territories, and for Arab-Jewish reconciliation.

Of the Other Zionist pioneers, Smilansky lived to make
a last passionate cry for justice to the Arabs shortly before
he died in 1953. The occasion was the passage by the
Knesset of the Land Requisition Law of 1953, which legal-
ized the expropriation of Arab lands. He wrote:

> When we came back to our country after having been
> evicted 2,000 years ago, we called ourselves "daring" and
> we rightly complained before the whole world that the
> gates of the country were shut. And now when they [Arab

refugees] dared to return to their country where they lived for 1,000 years before they were evicted or fled, they are called "infiltrees" and shot in cold blood. Where are you, Jews? Why do we not at least, with a generous hand, pay compensation to these miserable people? . . . And do we sin only against the refugees? Do we not treat the Arabs who remain with us as second-class citizens? . . . Did a single Jewish farmer raise his hand in the parliament in opposition to a law that deprived Arab peasants of their land? . . . How does it sit solitary, in the city of Jerusalem, the Jewish conscience?

Yet the center of moral gravity in the Zionist movement has moved steadily rightward. It is hard to find any trace of that prophetic ethic and that compassion in Prime Minister Begin. He symbolizes what Hans Kohn, another of the early bi-nationalists and a noted historian of nationalism, once called the moral " 'double-bookkeeping' which is so widely accepted in modern nationalism everywhere—a twofold scale of moral judgment, defining the same action as right for oneself but wrong in the neighbor."*

Nothing could point up more the contrast between the Smilansky view and Begin's than a footnote Begin appended to his story of the Deir Yassin massacre in his book *The Revolt: Story of the Irgun.* Begin defends the way the Irgun wiped out the Arab village of Deir Yassin near Jerusalem in the 1948 war as a military necessity. He even claims that the Irgun sacrificed the element of surprise to warn the villagers the attack was coming. But in a footnote

---

*This quotation and the quotation from Smilansky are taken from an article on "Zion and the Jewish National Idea" by Hans Kohn, published in 1958 in the *Menorah Journal,* now defunct but once the leading journal of Jewish culture in America.

he notes with undisguised satisfaction that the "wild tales of Irgun butchery" that resulted were so terrifying that Arabs throughout Palestine "were seized with limitless panic and started to flee for their lives. This mass flight soon turned into a mad, uncontrollable stampede. Of the about 800,000 Arabs who lived on the present territory of the state of Israel, only some 165,000 are still living there. The political and economic significance of this development can hardly be overestimated."* Neither can Begin's cold-blooded nationalistic calculation.

There is no greater, more fundamental and longstanding threat to Israel's survival than such an attitude toward the Arabs among whom the Israelis must find a way to live. Despite the changes wrought by thirty years of development and four wars, it is remarkable how little the situation has altered since the days when the Other Zionism was still pleading for a bi-nationalist solution. The choice is still either a life in common or a partitioned Palestine. Nothing could more dramatically demonstrate that the same old choice is inescapable than Begin's conduct in office. Though the government he heads controls all of Palestine west of the Jordan, he will not declare the occupied territories part of Israel, lest he thereby transform the present Jewish state into an Arab-Jewish state in which the Arabs might be, or soon become, the majority. Begin is equally unwilling to accept the only just alternative: to allow the Palestinians to build a life of their own in the so-called occupied territories. The Arabs fear that he plans instead to encroach on the land left them by expanding Jewish settlements and gradually force more Arabs to emigrate.

The Revolt (New York: Henry Schuman, 1951), p. 164.

No matter which the choice, the two peoples must live to-gether, either in the same Palestinian state or side by side in two Palestinian states. But either solution requires a re-vival of the Other Zionism, a recognition that two peoples —not one—occupy the same land and have the same rights. This is the path to reconciliation and reconciliation alone can guarantee Israel's survival. Israel can exhaust itself in new wars. It can commit suicide. It can pull down the pillars on itself and its neighbors. But it can live only by reviving that spirit of fraternity and justice and conciliation that the Prophets preached and the Other Zionism sought to apply. To go back and study the Other Zionism is, for dissidents like myself, to draw comfort in loneliness, to discover fresh sources of moral strength, and to find the secret of Israel's survival.

About the Author

I. F. Stone has become famous as a political analyst and reporter who has combined rare investigative ability with an outspoken commitment to principle and justice. He was born in Philadelphia in 1907, studied at the University of Pennsylvania, and launched his first publication in Haddonfield, New Jersey, at the age of fourteen. He has been a reporter, editorial writer, and columnist on the *Philadelphia Record, Philadelphia Inquirer, New York Post, PM, New York Star,* and *New York Daily Compass;* served as associate editor and Washington editor of *The Nation;* and was a contributing editor to the *New York Review of Books.* Between 1953 and 1971, he wrote and published his incomparable one-man newsletter, *I. F. Stone's Weekly,* which became the subject of a film. Recipient of numerous honorary degrees as well as L.I.U.'s George Polk Memorial Award and Columbia University's Journalism Award, he is the author of a dozen books and, since 1975, Distinguished Scholar in residence at American University.